W9-BXA-390

Black Hearts in Battersea

Black Hearts in Battersea

By Joan Aiken

Houghton Mifflin Company
Boston 1999

The text of this book is set in 12-point Apollo MT.

RNF ISBN 0-395-97115-2 PAP ISBN 0-395-97128-4

Manufactured in the United States of America
HAD 10 9 8 7 6 5 4 3 2 1

For Jessica AND *Joanna*

The action of this book takes place in the same period as that of *The Wolves of Willoughby Chase:* the reign of King James III, near the beginning of the nineteenth century, when England was still sadly plagued by wolves. A family tree of the Dukes of Battersea will be found on page 99.

1

On a fine warm evening in late summer, over a hundred years ago, a boy might have been seen leading a donkey across Southwark Bridge in the city of London. The boy, who appeared to be about fifteen, was bright-eyed and black-haired, and looked as if he had spent most of his life out of doors; he carried a knapsack, and wore rough, warm garments of frieze. Both boy and donkey seemed a little bewildered by the crowds round about them: the streets were thronged with people strolling in the sunshine after their day's work.

Halfway across the bridge the boy paused, took an extra turn of the donkey's halter round his wrist, and pulled out of his pouch a grubby and much-handled letter, which he proceeded to study.

"Come and stay with me for as long as you like, my dear Simon," he read, for the twentieth time. I have lately moved from Park Lane to lodgings that are less expensive, but sufficiently comfortable and commodious for us both. I have two rooms on the top floor of this house, which belongs to a Mr. and Mrs. Twite. The Twites are an unattractive family, but I see little enough of them. Moreover the windows command a handsome view of the river and St. Paul's Cathedral. I have spoken of you to Dr. Furnace, the Principal of the Art Academy in Chelsea where I sometimes study, and he is willing to accept you as a pupil. Through my visits to this Academy I have made another most interesting acquaintance to whom I wish to introduce you. More of this when we meet. Yours, Gabriel Field, M.D. P.S. Kindly remember me to Sir Willoughby and Lady Green, Miss Bonnie and Miss Sylvia Green, and all other friends in Yorkshire."

The letter was addressed from Rose Alley, Southwark, London.

The boy named Simon looked about him somewhat doubtfully and, after a moment's hesitation, accosted an elderly and rather frail-looking man with sparse locks who was walking slowly across the bridge.

"I wonder, sir," he said politely, "if you can direct me to Rose Alley? I believe it is not far from here."

The old man looked at him vaguely, stroking his beard with an unsteady hand.

"Rose Alley, now? Rose Alley, dear me? The name is indeed familiar . . ."

His hand stopped stroking and his eyes roamed vacantly past Simon. "Is that your beast?" he asked absently, his gaze lighting on the donkey. "Ah, I remember when I was a lad in the forest of Epping, I had a donkey; used to carry home bundles of firewood for a penny a load . . ." His voice trailed off.

"Rose Alley, sir," Simon said gently. "I am searching for the lodgings of a Dr. Field."

"Dr. Field, my boy?"

"Yes, sir, Dr. Gabriel Field."

"That name, too, seems familiar. Dear me, now, dear me, was it Dr. Field who put the bread poultice on my knee?" He advanced his knee and stared at it, seeming mildly surprised to find that the bread poultice was no longer there with Dr. Field's bill attached to it.

Simon, watching him, had not noticed an extremely dirty urchin who had been hovering near them. This individual, a sharp-looking boy of eleven or twelve who seemed to be dressed in nothing but one very large pair of trousers (he had cut holes in the sides for his arms) now jostled against Simon, contriving at the same moment to tread on his toes, flip his nose, and snatch Dr. Field's letter out of his hand. He then ran off, singing in a loud, rude manner,

"Simple Simon came to town,
Riding on a moke.
Donkey wouldn't go,
Wasn't that a joke?"

"Hey!" shouted Simon angrily. How did the boy know his name? "Give back that letter!"

He started in pursuit, but the boy, thumbing his nose derisively, crumpled up the letter and tossed it over the rail into the water. Then he disappeared into the crowd.

"Eh, deary me," said the old man, sighing in a discouraged manner. "The young people grow rougher and ruder every day. Now, what was it you were saying, my boy? You wanted the address of a Dr. Poultice? A strange name, a strange name—very. So far as I know there's no Dr. Poultice in these parts."

"No, Dr. *Field*—Dr. Gabriel Field in Rose Alley," said Simon, still vainly trying to catch a glimpse of the boy.

"Dr. Alley? Never heard of him. Now when I was a lad in the forest of Epping there was a Dr. Marble . . ."

Simon saw that he would get no good out of the old man, so he thanked him politely and walked on across the bridge.

"Did I hear you say you wanted Rose Alley?" said a voice in his ear. He turned with relief and saw a smallish, brisk-looking woman with pale blue eyes and pale sandy hair and a bonnet that was most ingeniously ornamented with vegetables. A small bunch of carrots decorated the brim, a couple of lettuce-leaves curled up rakishly at one side, and a veritable diadem of radishes was twined tastefully round the back.

"Yes, Dr. Field's lodgings in Rose Alley," said Simon, relieved to find someone who looked able to answer his question, for, though the little woman's bonnet was eccentric, her mouth was decided and her eyes were very sharp.

"Don't know any Dr. Field but I can tell you the best

way to get to Rose Alley," she said, and reeled off a set of directions so complicated that Simon had much ado to get them into his head. He thanked her and hurried on, repeating, "Two miles down Southwark Bridge Road, past the Elephant and Castle Inn, past Newington Butts, through Camberwell, then take a left turning and a right fork . . ."

But hey! he said to himself when he had gone half a mile, didn't Dr. Field say that from his window he had a view of the river Thames? And of St. Paul's Cathedral?

He turned round. St. Paul's Cathedral had been in view while he stood on Southwark Bridge. But now it was out of sight.

That woman must have been wrong, Simon thought, beginning to retrace his steps. She must have been thinking of some other Rose Alley. I'll go back until I am once more within sight of St. Paul's and the river, and ask somebody else. What a place this London is for confusion!

He presently reached the bridge once again, and this time was luckier in his adviser. A studious-looking young man with a bag of books said he was going to Rose Alley himself. He led Simon off the bridge around a couple of corners, and into a tiny cobbled lane giving directly onto the river front. There were but half a dozen tall, narrow, shabby houses on either side, and at the far end a patch of thistly grass sloped down to the water.

Simon had forgotten the number of the house where Dr. Field lodged, but when he asked which belonged to Mr. and Mrs. Twite the young man pointed to the last house on the right, Number Eight, which stood with its back to the bridge and its side to the river.

Simon tethered his donkey to some broken railings and knocked on the door, which was in need of a coat of paint.

For a long time there was no reply. He knocked again, louder. At that, a window flew open and a child's head popped out.

"There's nobody in but me," she snapped. "Whose donkey is that?"

"Mine. Is this the house of Mr. and Mrs. Twite?"

"Yes it is. I'm Miss Twite," the brat said with a haughty air. "What d'you want?"

"I'm looking for Dr. Field."

"There's no Dr. Field here. Can your donkey gallop? What's its name?"

"Caroline. Do you mean Dr. Field is out?" The child looked thoroughly unreliable and Simon was not sure whether to believe her.

"Can your donkey gallop?" she repeated.

"If you'll come down and answer the door I'll give you a ride on her," said Simon. She vanished like lightning and reappeared in the doorway. She was a shrewish-looking little creature of perhaps eight or nine, with sharp eyes of a pale washed-out blue and no eyebrows or eyelashes to speak of. Her straw-colored hair was stringy and sticky with jam and she wore a dirty satin dress two sizes too small for her.

"Is Dr. Field out? Do you know when he'll be back?"

Simon said again.

She took no notice of his question but walked up to the donkey and untied it. "Lift me on its back," she ordered. Simon good-naturedly did so, urged the reluctant Caroline to a trot, and led her to the end of Rose Alley and back. Miss Twite hung on to the saddle with loud exclamations.

"Mind out! Not so fast, you're shaking me! She's bumping, make her slow down! Oo, your saddle's hard!"

When they arrived back at Number Eight she cried, "Give me another ride!"

"Not till you tell me when Dr. Field will be back."

"Don't know."

"Well, where are your father and mother?"

"They've gone to Vauxhall Gardens with Penny and Grandpa and Aunt Tinty and they won't be back till midnight past."

"Why aren't you with them?"

"Acos I threw Penny's hat on the fire," she said, bursting into giggles. "Oo, how they did scold! Pa walloped me with a slipper, leastways he tried to, and Ma said I mightn't go out, and Penny pinched me. Spiteful cat."

"Who's minding you?"

"I'm minding myself. Give me another ride!"

"Not just now. The donkey's tired, she and I have come all the way from Yorkshire this week. If you're good you shall have another ride later, perhaps." Simon was learning cunning. But Miss Twite looked at him with a knowing, weary eye and said, "Gammon! I know yer 'later perhaps!'"

"Would you like to give the donkey some carrots?" Simon said, visited with inspiration.

"Don't mind."

He pulled a handful of carrots out of the pannier and broke them up.

Miss Twite was delighted with the privilege of feeding Caroline, and almost shed her world-weary air. Seeing her absorbed, Simon quietly walked through the front door of the house and up a steep and dirty flight of stairs, past several landings. At the top of the house two doors faced one another. Simon remembered that Dr. Field had said there were two rooms; doubtless both of these were his. But no reply came from either door when he tapped; it appeared that the child had been speaking the truth and Dr. Field was indeed out.

It could surely do no harm to wait for him here, however, Simon thought. By this time he was decidedly fatigued, and a kitten, which had been asleep in his knapsack, at this moment woke up and mewed to be released.

Simon opened one of the doors and looked through into the room beyond.

As soon as he saw the window he recognized the view that Dr. Field had described—the river, and Southwark Bridge, and an expanse of mud gleaming pink in the sunset below the tethered barges. Beyond towered the dome of St. Paul's. But, strangely enough, the room, which had a faintly familiar smell, did not contain a single stick of furniture.

"Perhaps this room is for me and I am to buy my own

things," Simon thought, and recrossed the landing, remembering with a grin Dr. Field's previous lodgings in Park Lane, where painting equipment, easels, palettes, and bottles of turpentine jostled pills and medicine phials, while a skeleton lounged on the sofa.

But the other room, too, was bare. It did contain a little furniture—a bed, table, and chair, and a worn strip of drugget on the floor. But there were no covers on the bed and it was plain that this room, too, was unoccupied.

Simon scratched his head. Could he have made a mistake? But no, Dr. Field had distinctly written "Mr. and Mrs. Twite, Rose Alley, Southwark," and here, sure enough, was the Twite house in Rose Alley. Here was the top room with the view of St. Paul's. The only thing lacking was Dr. Field himself. Perhaps he had not yet moved from his other lodgings? And yet Simon had received the letter with the new address a full two months ago, and had then written to Rose Alley saying when he proposed to arrive. Could something have changed or delayed the doctor's plans? Simon ran down the stairs again, resolved on trying to get a little more help from young Miss Twite.

He arrived none too soon for poor Caroline. Having finished the carrots—Simon observed traces of carrot on the child's face and deduced that the donkey had not received a full ration—Miss Twite had contrived to clamber onto Caroline's back from the railings. Using a rusty old umbrella she was urging the donkey at a fast trot along Rose Alley.

Simon ran after them and grabbed the bridle.

"You little wretch!" he remarked. "Didn't you hear me

say Caroline was tired?"

"Fiddlesticks!" said Miss Twite. "There's plenty of go in her yet." She raised the umbrella, and Simon twitched it neatly out of her hand.

"So there would be in you if I beat you with an umbrella."

"Are you going to? I'll tell my Pa if you do!" Miss Twite eyed him alertly.

Simon couldn't help laughing, she looked so like an ugly, scrawny little bird, ready to hop out of the way if danger threatened. He led Caroline back to her pasturage and dumped Miss Twite on the steps of Number Eight.

"Now then, tell me once and for all—where is Dr. Field?"

"What Dr. Field? I don't know any Dr. Field!"

"You said just now he was out."

"I only said that to get a ride," said Miss Twite, bursting into a fit of laughter and throwing herself from side to side in the ecstasy of her amusement. "I've never met Dr. Field in my life."

"But he was going to move here—I'm almost sure he *did* move here," said Simon, remembering the words in the doctor's letter—"The Twites are an unattractive family but I see little enough of them"—didn't that sound as if he were already moved in? And this specimen of the Twite family was unattractive enough, heaven knows!

"There's no Dr. Field living here and never has been," said the child definitely.

"Who lives in your top rooms?"

"They're empty."

"Are you sure Dr. Field isn't coming soon?"

"I tell you, no!" She stamped her foot. "Stop talking about Dr. Field! Can I have another ride?"

"No, you can*not*," said Simon, exasperated. He wondered what he had better do.

If only Mr. or Mrs. Twite were here, they might be able to throw some light on this puzzling situation.

"Is that a kitty in your knapsack?" said Miss Twite. "Why do you keep it there? Let it out. Let me see it!"

"If I let you see it," said Simon cautiously, "will you let me stay the night? I could sleep in your top room. I'll pay you of course," he added quickly.

She hesitated, chewing a strand of her stringy hair. "Dunno what Ma or Pa would say. They might beat me. And what 'bout the donkey? Where'll she go?"

"I'll find a place for her." There was a row of little shops round the corner, greengrocer's, butcher's, dairy—Simon thought it probable that he could find lodgings for Caroline behind one of them. He was not going to risk leaving her tethered in the street with this child about.

"Will you promise to give me another ride tomorrow?"

"Yes."

"But Pa only lets by the week," she said swiftly. "It's twelve-and-six the week, boots and washing extry, and a shilling a day fires in winter. If you stayed the week you could give me a ride every day."

"All right, you little madam," said Simon, rapidly reckoning how long his small stock of money would last.

"Hand over the twelve-and-six, then."

"Not likely! I'll give that to your father."

She accepted this defeat with a grin and said, "Show me the kitty, then."

"First I want to buy some food and find a place for the donkey. You'd better be putting sheets on the bed." Miss Twite made a grimace but trailed indoors, leaving the front door ajar.

When he had bought milk and eggs at the dairy Simon arranged to stable Caroline with the milk roundsman's pony for half a crown a week, this sum to be reduced if she was ever borrowed for the milk deliveries. Simon was not quite satisfied with this arrangement—the sour-looking dairywoman had too strong a resemblance to young Miss Twite for his taste and he wondered if they were related—but it would do for the time.

He purchased a quantity of cold ham and a loaf of bread and then returned to Rose Alley where the door still stood open.

Surprisingly enough, young Miss Twite had taken a pair of sheets and blankets up to the top room and was rather carelessly throwing them over the bed.

"*Now* let's see the kitty," she said.

Simon's kitten was equally eager to be let out from its traveling-quarters, and gave a mighty stretch before mewing loudly for bread and milk.

"I suppose you're hungry too," Simon said, noticing Miss Twite's hopeful looks at the loaf.

"Aren't I jist? Ma said I was to miss my dinner on

account of burning Penny's hat—spiteful thing."

"Who's Penny?" Simon asked, cutting her a slice.

"My sister. Oo, she's a horrible girl. She's sixteen. Her real name's Pen-el-o-pe." She mouthed it out disgustedly.

"What's yours?"

"Dido."

"I never heard that name before."

"It's after a barge. So's Penny's. Can I have another bit?"

He gave her another, noticing that she had already eaten most of the ham.

"Can I take the kitty down and play in the street?"

"No, I'm going to bed now, and so's the kitty. Tell your father that I've taken the room for a week and I'm waiting for Dr. Field."

"I tell you," she said, turning in the doorway for emphasis, "there *ain't* any Dr. Field. There never *has* been any Dr. Field."

Simon shrugged and waited till she had gone. Then he went across into the room that faced onto the river and stared out of the window. It was nearly dark by now, and the opposite bank glittered with lights, some low down by the water, some high up on St. Paul's. Barges glided upstream with the tide, letting out mournful hoots. Dr. Field had been here, Dr. Field had seen this view. Dr. Field must be somewhere. But where?

Simon soon went to sleep, though the mattress was hard and the bedding scanty. At about one in the morning, however, he and the kitten, who was asleep on his chest, were awakened by very loud singing and the slamming of several doors downstairs.

Presently, as the singer apparently mounted several flights of stairs, the words of the song could be distinguished:

"My Bonnie lies over the North Sea,
My Bonnie lies over in Hanover,
My Bonnie lies over the North Sea
Oh, why won't they bring that young man over?
Bring back, bring back,
Oh, bring back my Georgie to me, to me . . ."

Simon realized that the singer must be one of the Georgians, or Hanoverians as they were sometimes called, who wanted to dethrone King James and bring back the pretender, young Prince George of Hanover. He couldn't help wondering if the singer were aware of his rashness in thus making known his political feelings, for, since the long and hard-fought Hanoverian wars had secured King James III on the throne, the mood of the country was strongly anti-Georgian and anybody who proclaimed his sympathy for the pretender was liable to be ducked in the nearest horse-pond, if not haled off to the Tower for treason.

"Abednego!" cried a sharp female voice. "Abednego, will you hold your hush this instant! Hold your hush and come downstairs—I've your nightcap a-warming and a hot salamander in the bed—and besides, you'll wake the neighbors!"

"Neighbors be blowed!" roared the voice of the singer. "What do I care about the neighbors? I need solitude. I need to commune with Nature. I'm going to sleep up in the top room—mind I'm not called in the morning till eleven past when you can bring me a mug of warm ale and a piece of toast."

The steps came, very unsteadily, up the last flight of stairs. The kitten prudently retired under the bed just before the door burst open and a man lurched into the room.

He carried a candle which, after several false tries, he succeeded in placing on the table, muttering to himself, "Cursed Picts and Jacobins! They've moved it again. Every time I leave the house those Picts and Jacobins creep in and shift the furniture."

He turned toward the bed and for the first time saw Simon sitting up and staring at him.

"A Pict!" he shrieked. "Help! Ella! There's a Pict got into the house! Bring the poker and the ax! Quick!"

"Don't talk fiddlesticks," the lady called up the stairs. "There's nothing up top that shouldn't be there—as I should know. Didn't I scrub up there with Bath brick for days together? I'll Pict you!"

"Are you Mr. Twite?" Simon said, hoping to reassure the man.

"Ella! It speaks! It's a Pict and it speaks!"

"Hold your hush or I'll lambast you with the salamander!" she shouted.

But as the man made no attempt to hold his hush but continued to shriek and to beseech Ella to bring the poker and the ax, there came at length the sound of more feet on the stairs and a lady entered the room carrying, not the ax, but a warming pan filled with hot coals, which she shook threateningly.

"Come along down this minute, Abednego, or I'll give you such a rousting!" she snapped, and then she saw Simon. Her mouth and eyes opened very wide, and she almost dropped the warming pan, but, retaining her hold on it, shortened her grip and advanced toward the bed in a very intimidating manner.

"And who might *you* be?" she said.

"If you please, ma'am, my name is Simon, and I rented your top rooms from your daughter Dido this evening—if you're Mrs. Twite, that is?" Simon said.

"I'm Mrs. Twite, all right," she said ominously. "And what's more, *I'm* the one that lets rooms in this house, and so I'll tell that young good-for-nothing baggage. Renting room to all and sundry! We might have been murdered in our beds!"

Simon reflected that it looked much more as if he would be the one to be murdered in his bed. Mrs. Twite was standing beside the bed with the warming pan held over him menacingly; at any moment, it seemed, she might drop the whole panful of hot coals on his legs.

She was a large, imposing woman, with a quantity of gingerish fair hair all done up in curlpapers so that her head was a strange and fearsome shape.

In order to show his good intentions as quickly as possible Simon got out his money, which he had stowed under the pillow, and offered Mrs. Twite five half crowns.

"I understand the room is twelve-and-six a week," he said.

"Boots and washing extra!" she snapped, her eyes going as sharp as bradawls at sight of the money. "And it'll be another half crown for arriving at dead of night and nearly frightening Mr. Twite into convulsions. And even then I'm not sure the room's free. What do you say, Mr. Twite?"

Mr. Twite had calmed down as soon as his lady entered, and had wandered to a corner where he stood balancing himself alternately on his toes and his heels, singing in a plaintive manner,

"Picts and pixies, come and stay, come and stay,
Come, come, and pay, pay, pay."

When his wife asked his opinion he answered, "Oh, very well, my dear, if he has money he can stay, *I've* no objection if you are satisfied. What is a Pict or two under one's roof, to be sure?"

Simon handed over the extra half crown and was just about to raise the matter of Dr. Field when Mr. Twite burst into song again (to the tune, this time, of "I Had a Good Home and I Left") and caroled,

"A Pict, a Pict, she rented the room to a Pict,
And I think she ought to be kicked."

"Come along, my dove," he said, interrupting himself, "the Pict wants to get some sleep and I'm for the downy myself." Picking up the candle he urged his wife to the door.

"I thought you wanted to commune with Nature," she said acidly, pocketing the money.

"Nature will have to wait till the morning," Mr. Twite replied, with a magnificent gesture toward the window which had the unfortunate effect of blowing out the candle. The Twites made their way downstairs by the glow of the warming pan.

Simon and the kitten settled to sleep once more and there were no further disturbances.

2

When Simon woke next morning he lay for a few minutes wondering where he was. It seemed strange to wake in a bed, in a room, in the middle of a city. He was used to waking in a cave in the woods, or, in summer, to sleeping out under the trees, being roused by the birds to lie looking up at the green canopy overhead. He felt uneasy so far away from the grass and trees of the forest home where he had lived for the past five years.

Outside, in the street, he could hear wheels and voices; the kitten was awake and mewing for its breakfast. After Simon had fed it the last of the milk he wandered across the landing to the empty room and gazed out of the window. The tide was nearly full, and the Thames was a bustle of activity. Simon watched the shipping, absorbed, until a whole series of church clocks striking culminated in the solemn boom of St. Paul's itself, and reminded him that he could not stand here all day gazing while time slipped by. It was still needful to discover Dr. Field's whereabouts, and to earn some money.

Kind, wealthy Sir Willoughby Green, who had befriended Simon in Yorkshire, had offered to pay his art-school fees, but Simon had no intention of being beholden if he could avoid it, and proposed to look for work which would provide enough money for his tuition as well as food and rent. He had a considerable fund of quiet pride, and had purposely waited to leave Willoughby Chase until the Green family was away on a visit. Thus he had been spared a sad farewell, and had also avoided the risk of hurting Sir Willoughby's feelings by refusing the money which he knew that liberal-hearted gentleman would have pressed on him.

Munching a piece of bread, Simon tucked the kitten into the bosom of his frieze jacket; then he ran softly downstairs. The house was silent—evidently the Twites were still asleep. Simon resolved that he would not wait till they woke to question them about Dr. Field, but would go to the Academy of Art which he was to attend—where Dr. Field also studied—to ask for the doctor's address. Unfortunately Simon did not know the name of the academy, but he remembered that it was in Chelsea.

He stole past the closed doors of the Twites, resolving that when he returned in the evening he would move the furniture from the room where he had slept into the one overlooking the river; it had a pleasanter view, and appeared to be in a superior state of cleanliness.

Opening the front door Simon found Dido Twite sitting on the front steps, kicking her heels discontentedly. She was wearing the same stained dress that she had had on yesterday, and did not appear to have washed her face or brushed her hair since Simon had last seen her.

"Hallo!" she said alertly. "Where are you going?"

"Out," said Simon. He had no intention of retailing all his doings to her and having them discussed by the Twite family.

Dido's face fell. "What about my donkey ride?" she said, looking at him from under where her brows would have been had she had any.

Although she was an unattractive brat, she had such a forlorn, neglected air that Simon's heart softened. "All right," he said, "I'll get Caroline and give you a ride if you'll do something for me while I'm fetching her."

"What?" said Dido suspiciously.

"Wash your face." He went whistling up the street.

After he had given Dido her ride he asked, "What time is your father likely to get up?"

"Not till noon—perhaps not till three or four. Pa works evenings and sleeps all day—if Penny or I wake him he throws his hoboy at us."

Simon could not imagine what a hoboy might be, but it seemed plain that no information was to be had from Mr. Twite until the evening.

"Well, good-by. I'll see you when I come home. What do you do with yourself all day? Do you go to school?"

"No," she said peevishly. "Sometimes Pa teaches me the hoboy or Aunt Tinty sets me sums. Uncle Buckle used to teach me but he doesn't any more. Mostly I does tasks for Ma—peel the spuds, sweep the stairs, stoke the furnace—"

"Furnace!" exclaimed Simon. "That was the name!"

"What name?"

"Oh, nothing that concerns you. The principal of the art academy where I am to learn painting."

He had thrown the information over his shoulder as he walked away, not thinking that it could be of any possible interest to Dido Twite. He would have been surprised to see the sudden flash of alert calculation in her eyes.

Simon asked his way through the streets till he reached Chelsea—no very great distance, as it proved. Here he inquired of a man in the uniform of a beadle where he would find an academy of art presided over by a Dr. Furnace.

The beadle scratched his head.

"Dr. Furnace?" he said. "Can't say as I recall the name."

Simon's heart sank. Was Dr. Furnace to prove as elusive as Dr. Field? But then the beadle turned and shouted, "Dan!" to a man who was just emerging from an arched gateway leading a horse and gaily painted dust-cart with a cracked wheel.

"Hallo?" replied this man. "What's the row?"

"Young cove here wants Furnace's Art Academy. Know what he means?"

Both men turned and stared at Simon. The man called Dan, who was dressed in moleskin clothes from cap to leggings, slowly chewed a straw to its end, spat, and then said, "Furnace's Academy? Ah. I know what he means. He means Rivière's."

"Ah," said the beadle wisely. "That's what you mean,

me boy. You means Rivière's."

"Is that far from here?" said Simon, his hopes rising.

"Matter o' ten minutes' walk," said Dan. "Going that way meself. I'll take you."

"Thank you, sir."

They strolled off, Dan leading the horse.

"I'm going to me brother-in-law's," he explained. "Does the smithying and wheelwrighting for the parish. Nice line o' business."

Simon was interested. He had worked for a blacksmith himself and knew a fair amount about the wheelwright's trade.

"There must be plenty of customers for a wheelwright in London," he said, looking about him. "I've never seen so many different kinds of carriages before. Where I come from it's mostly closed coaches and farm carts."

"Countryfied sort o' stuff," said Dan pityingly. "No art in it—and mind you, there's a lot of art in the coachmaker's trade. You get the *length* without the 'ighth, it looks poky and old-fashioned, to my mind, but, contrariwise, you get the 'ighth without enough body and it looks a reg'lar hurrah's-nest. Now *there's* a lovely bit o' bodywork—see that barouche coming along—the plum-colored one with the olive-drab outwork? Ah, very racy, that is—Duke o' Battersea's trot-box; know it well. Seen it at me brother-in-law's for repair: cracked panel."

Simon turned and saw an elegantly turned-out vehicle in which was seated an elderly lady dressed in the height of fashion with waterfalls of diamonds ornamenting her apple-peel satin gown, and a tremendous ostrich-plume headdress. She was accompanied by a pretty young girl who held a reticule, two billiard cues, a large shopping basket, and a small spaniel.

"Why!" Simon exclaimed. "That's *Sophie!*"

His voice rang across the street and the young girl turned her head sharply. But just then a high closed carriage came between Simon and the barouche and, a succession of other traffic following after, no second view of the girl could be obtained.

"I know that girl! She's a friend of mine!" Simon said, overjoyed. He looked at Dan with shining eyes.

"Ah. Duchess's lady's-maid, maybe? Nice-looking young gel. Very good position—good family to work for. Duke very affable sort o' gentleman—when he comes out o' those everlasting experiments of his. Bugs, chemicals, mice—queer setout for a lord. But his lady's a proper lady, so I've been told. O' course young Lord Bakerloo ain't up to much."

"Where does he live—the Duke of Battersea?" asked Simon, who had not been paying much attention.

"Battersea Castle o' course—when the family's in London. Places in the country too, nat'rally. Dorset, Yorkshire—that where you met the gel? Now, here's me brother-in-law's establishment, and, down by the river, that big place with the pillars is Rivière's."

Dan's brother-in-law's place was almost as impressive as the art academy beyond. Inside the big double gates (over which ran the legend "Cobb's Coaches," in gold) was a wide yard containing every conceivable kind of coach, carriage, phaeton, barouche, landau, chariot, and curricle, in every imaginable state of disrepair. A shed at the side contained a forge, with bellows roaring and sparks blowing, while elsewhere lathes turned, carpenters hammered, and chips flew.

"Do you suppose I could get work here?" Simon asked impulsively. "Of an evening—when I've finished at the academy?"

"No 'arm in asking, is there? Always plenty to do at Sam Cobb's, that I do know. Depends what you can do, dunnit?"

Dan led his dust-cart through the gates and then lifted up his voice and bawled, *"Sam!"*

A large, cheerful man came toward them.

"Why, bless me!" he exclaimed. "If it's not old Dan back again. I don't know what you do to your cart, Dan, I don't indeed. *I* believe it's fast driving. *I* believe you're out of an evening carriage-racing on the Brighton Road. You can't expect the parish dust-carts to stand up to it, Dan, no you can't, me boy."

Dan took these pleasantries agreeably, and asked after his sister Flossie. Then he said, "Here's a young cove, Sam, as wants a bit of evening work. Any use to you?"

"Any use to me?" said Mr. Cobb, summing up Simon with a shrewd but friendly eye. "Depends what he can do, eh? Looks a well-set-up young 'un. What can you do, young 'un? Can you carpenter?"

"Yes," said Simon.

"Done any blacksmith's work?"

"Yes," said Simon.

"Used to horses?"

"Yes," said Simon.

"Ever tried your hand at ornamental painting?" said Mr. Cobb, gesturing toward a little greengrocer's cart, newly and beautifully ornamented with roses and lettuces. "This sort o' thing? Or emblazoning?" He waved at a carriage with a coat-of-arms on the panel.

"I can paint a bit," said Simon. "That's why I've come to London—to study painting."

"Proper all-rounder, ennee?" said Mr. Cobb, rolling his eyes in admiration.

"You'd best take him on, Sam, then you'll be able to retire," Dan remarked.

"Well, I like a young 'un who has confidence in hisself, I like a bit o' spunk. And dear knows there's plenty of work. Tell you what, young 'un, you come round here this evening, fiveish, and I'll see what you can do. Agreeable?"

"Very, thank you sir," Simon answered cheerfully. "And thank *you,* for setting me on my way," he said to Dan, who winked at him in a friendly manner.

"Good-by, young 'un. Now then, Dan," said Mr. Cobb, "it's early, to be sure, but there's such a nip in the air these misty mornings; what do you say to a little drop of Organ-Grinder's Oil?"

Simon felt somewhat nervous, as he approached the academy, but was encouraged to find that on a nearer view it presented a less imposing aspect. Some ingenious spirit had hit on the notion of suspending clotheslines between the Grecian columns supporting the roof, and from these dangled a great many socks, shirts, and other garments, while all round the marble fountain in front of the academy knelt or squatted young persons of both sexes busily engaged in washing various articles of apparel.

Simon approached a young man who was scrubbing a pair of red socks with a bar of yellow soap, and said, "Can you tell me, please, where I shall find Dr. Furnace?"

The young man rinsed his socks, held them up, sniffed them, glanced at the sun, and said, "About ten o'clock, is it? He'll be having breakfast. In his room on the first floor."

He sniffed his socks again, remarked that they still smelt of paint, and set to rubbing them once more.

Simon walked on, wondering if the young man kept his paints in his socks. In the doorway a sudden recollection hit him. Paint! That was the smell that had seemed so familiar in the top front room at Mrs. Twite's. Of course it was paint! Then—Simon stopped, assailed by suspicion—was that why Mrs. Twite had been scrubbing with Bath brick? To remove the smell of paint? Why?

Pondering this, Simon sat down on the first convenient object he found—a stone statue of a lion, half finished—to unravel the matter a little further.

Dido said Dr. Field had not been at the Twites'. But the

rooms were as he had described them, the address was as he had given it, and the room smelt of paint, which suggested that he had occupied it.

Perhaps, Simon thought, perhaps he had fallen out with the Twites—had had something stolen, or found the house too dirty, or objected to being woken at one in the morning by Hanoverian songs. He had complained, taken his leave, and moved away. The Twites, annoyed at losing a lodger, had contrived an elaborate pretense that no Dr. Field had ever lived with them . . .

Somehow Simon found it hard to believe this. For one thing, Dr. Field was far from fussy, and, provided he was furnished with privacy and a good light for painting, was unlikely to object if his neighbors practiced cannibalism or played the bass drum all day so long as they let him alone. And, secondly, why should the Twites bother to make such a pretense about a trivial matter? Half a dozen people, neighbors, patients, local tradesmen, would be able to give their story the lie.

Then it occurred to Simon that he had not yet heard what Mr. or Mrs. Twite had to say; he had only had Dido's version. Perhaps the whole mystery was just her nonsense, and when he got back that night he would be handed a piece of paper with Dr. Field's address on it.

Cheered by this reasonable notion, Simon stood up and crossed the entrance hall. A large double flight of marble stairs faced him, and between them stood a statue of a man in a huge wig, dressed in knee breeches and a painter's smock. He held a marble paintbrush and was engaged in painting a marble picture on a marble easel. The back of the easel bore an inscription:

MARIUS RIVIÈRE
1759–1819
FOUNDED THIS ACADEMY

Simon noticed, when he was high enough up the stairs to be able to look over the marble gentleman's shoulder, that someone had painted a picture of a pink pig wearing a blue bow on the marble canvas.

Opposite the top of the stairs he saw a door labeled "Principal." Rather timidly he knocked on it, and an impatient voice shouted, *"Alors—entrez!"*

Walking in, Simon found himself in a medium-sized room that was overpoweringly warm and smelt strongly of garlic and coffee and turpentine. The warmth came from two braziers full of glowing charcoal, on one of which a kettle steamed briskly. The room was so untidy—littered with stacks of canvases, baskets of fruit, wood carvings, strings of onions hanging from the ceiling, easels with pictures on them, statues—that at first Simon did not see the little man who had told him to come in. But after a moment the same irascible voice said, *"Eh bien!* Shut the door, if you please and declare yourself!"

"Are—are you Dr. Furnace, please, sir?" Simon said hesitantly.

"Furrneaux, if you please, *Furrneaux*—I cannot endure the English pronunciation."

Dr. Furnace or Furneaux was hardly more than three feet six inches high, and extraordinarily whiskery. As he rose up from behind his desk he reminded Simon irresistibly of a prawn. His whiskers waved, his hands waved, a pair of snapping black eyes took in every inch of Simon from his dusty shoes to the kitten's face poking inquisitively out of his jacket.

"And so, and so?" Dr. Furneaux said impatiently. "Who may you be?"

"If you please, sir, my name is Simon, and I believe Dr. Field spoke about me—"

"Ah, yes, Gabriel Field. A boy named Simon. *Attendez*—"

Dr. Furneaux waved his antennae imperatively, darted over to a cupboard, returned with a coffeepot, tipped coffee into it from a blue paper bag, poured in hot water, produced cups from a tea chest and sugar from another blue paper bag.

"Now we wait a moment. A boy named Simon, yes. Gabriel Field mentioned you, yes. In a moment I shall see what you can do. You are hungry?" he said, looking sternly at Simon. "Take the bread off that brazier—zere, blockhead!—and find some plates and some butter. In ze brown jar, of course!" as Simon, bewildered, looked uncertainly about him. The brown earthenware jar resembled something from *The Arabian Nights* and could easily have held Ali Baba and a couple of thieves.

"So, now we eat," said Dr. Furneaux, breaking eight inches off a loaf shaped like a rolling pin and handing it to Simon. "I will pour ze coffee in a moment. Tell me about my good friend Dr. Gabriel Field—how is it wiss him?"

"Dr. Field?" Simon stammered, absently taking a large bite of the crisp bread which flew into crumbs all round him, "but—haven't you seen him? I thought he would be here."

"Not since my *jour-de-fête* in July," said Dr. Furneaux, carefully pouring coffee into two cups and handing one to Simon.

"But then, but—"

"He said you were to live wiss him. Are you not, then?"

"He seems to have moved. He is not at the address he sent—"

"Chose assez étonnante," Dr. Furneaux muttered to himself. "Can Dr. Field be in debt? Escaping his creditors? Or in prison? He would have told me . . ."

"He wrote inviting me to come and live with him, sir," Simon said. "He would have said if he was planning to move—"

"Well, no doubt he has been called away on ze private affairs. He will return. One sing is certain, he will come back here. Now, you have eaten? Ze little one, he has eaten too?" Dr. Furneaux nodded benevolently at the kitten which was licking up some crumbs of bread and butter from the dusty floor. "It is well. To work, zen! I wish to see you draw." He handed Simon a stick of charcoal.

"Yes, sir." Simon took the charcoal with a trembling hand. "Wh-where shall I draw?"

Dr. Furneaux's whiskered gaze roved round the room. There was not a clean canvas nor an empty space in it.

"Draw on zat wall," the doctor said, waving at the wall to his right, which was invitingly bare and white.

"All over it, sir?"

"Of course."

"What shall I draw?"

"Oh—anysing you have seen in ze last few days."

As usual when Simon started drawing, he was rapt away into a world of his own. People knocked and entered and consulted Dr. Furneaux, waited for assistance, went away again; some of them stared at Simon, others took no notice. Dr. Furneaux himself came and went darting out to conduct a class, or back to criticize the efforts of a private pupil. At intervals he made more coffee, from time to time offered a cup of it—or a piece of bread, apple, grape, or sausage—to Simon. He ignored Simon's work, preferring, apparently, to wait till it was finished.

Toward noon a boy a little younger than Simon came in escorted by a tall, thin man.

"Man dieu!" Dr. Furneaux groaned to himself at sight of them. Then he stood up and waved them forward.

"My dear young Justin—my dearest friend's grandson! And the sage Mr. Buckle. *Enchanté de vous voir.* Mr. Buckle—do yourself ze kindness to sit down. Let us see what you have been working at ziss week, my dear Justin."

The boy did not speak, but hunched his shoulders and looked depressed, while the man addressed as Mr. Buckle—a sandy-haired, pale-eyed individual dressed in rusty black—laid a small pile of drawings on the desk.

Neither the man nor the boy took any notice of Simon,

who observed that the boy looked positively ill with apprehension as Dr. Furneaux examined his work. He was a sickly-looking lad, very richly dressed, but the olive-green velvet of his jacket went badly with his pale, spotty cheeks, and the plumed hat which he had taken off revealed lank, stringy hair.

It was plain that he wished himself a thousand miles away.

Dr. Furneaux looked slowly and carefully through the pile of drawings. Once or twice he seemed about to burst out with some remark, but restrained himself; when he reached the last, however, his feelings became too much for him and he exploded with rage.

"How can you, how *can* you bring such stuff to show to *me,* Jean-Jacques Furneaux, Principal of ze Rivière Academie? Zis, *zis* is what I sink of zese *abominable* drawings!"

With considerable difficulty he tore the whole batch across and across, scattering pieces of paper all about him, his whiskers quivering, his eyes snapping with rage. Although so small, he was a formidable spectacle. The boy, Justin, seemed ready to melt into the ground with terror as bits of paper flew like autumn leaves. Simon watched with awe and apprehension. If Dr. Furneaux was so severe with a familiar pupil, grandson of an old friend, what was his own reception likely to be?

The only person who thoroughly enjoyed the scene was the kitten, who darted out and chased the fluttering scraps of paper around Dr. Furneaux's feet. The sight of him appeared to calm the fiery little principal. He stopped hissing and stamping, stared at the kitten, snapped his fingers, took several deep breaths, and walked briskly two or three times up and down the room, neatly avoiding all the obstacles. At last he said, "I have been too harsh. I do not mean to alarm you, my dear boy. No, no, I hope I treat my best friend's grandson better zan zat. But zere must, zere *must* be a painter hidden in ze grandson of Marius Rivière. We shall wr-rrench him out, *n'est-ce-pas?* Now—you shall draw somesing simple—"

His eye roamed about the room and lit on the kitten. "You shall draw zat cat! Of the most simple, no? Here—" He swept everything, plates, bread, papers, and ink off his desk in disorder, found a stack of clean paper, and beckoned to Justin. "Here, my dear boy. Here is charcoal, here is crayon. Now—*draw!* I shall return in two hours' time. Come, my dear Mr. Buckle, Justin will be easier if we leave him alone."

He took the arm of Mr. Buckle, who moved reluctantly toward the door.

"Who is that?" he asked sourly, pointing to the legs of Simon, who was lying on his stomach behind the Arabian Nights jar, drawing cobblestones.

"Zat?" Dr. Furneaux shrugged. "Nobody. A boy from nowhere. He will not disturb Justin—his mind is engr-rossed in drawing."

The door closed behind them.

Simon felt sorry for Justin—it seemed unreasonable to expect the boy to be a painter just because his grandfather had been one and founded the Academy. People, surely, did not always take after their grandfathers? Perhaps I'm lucky, Simon thought for the first time, not to know who my parents or grandparents were.

After working diligently for another half hour he stood up and stretched, to rest his cramped muscles. The kitten greeted him with a loud squeak of pleasure and ran up his leg. But the boy Justin took no notice—he was sitting at the desk, slumped forward with his face in his hands, the picture of dejection. He had not even started to draw.

"I say, cheer up," Simon said sympathetically. "It can't be as bad as that, surely?"

Justin hunched one shoulder away from him.

"Oh, *you're* all right," he said with the rudeness of misery. "Nobody cares how *you* draw. But just because my grandfather was a painter and started this place, everyone expects me to be wonderful. Why should I learn to paint? I'm going to be a duke. Dukes don't paint."

"I say, are you though?" Simon said with interest. "I've never met a duke."

"And I daresay you never will," Justin said listlessly. Just at that moment the kitten climbed across from Simon's leg to the desk and began playing with a ball of charcoal eraser. Justin made a rather hopeless attempt at sketching it, but it would not oblige him by staying still, and, after jabbing a few crude scrawls, he exclaimed furiously, "Oh, curse and confound the little brute!" and hurled the charcoal across the room. The kitten sat down at once and stared at him with large reproving eyes.

"Quick, now's your chance while he's still," Simon urged encouragingly. "Try again."

"I can't draw live things!" snapped Justin. "A kitten hasn't any shape, it's all fuzzy!" He angrily scribbled a matchstick cat—four legs, two ears, and a tail—then rubbed it out with his fist and drew the same fist over his eyes, leaving a damp, charcoaly smear on his cheek.

"No," said Simon patiently, "*look* at the kitten, look at its shape and then draw that—never mind if what you draw doesn't look like a cat. Here—" He picked up another bit of charcoal and, without taking the tip off the paper, quickly drew an outline—quite carelessly, it seemed, but Justin gasped as the shape of the kitten fairly leaped out of the paper. "I could never do that," he said with grudging admiration.

"Yes you could—try!"

Advising, coaxing, half guiding Justin's hand, Simon made him produce a rough, free drawing which was certainly a great deal better than his previous work.

"You ought to feel the kitten all over," Simon suggested. "Feel the way its bones go. It looks fluffy but it's not like a wig—it has a hard shape under the fur."

"I shall never be able to draw," Justin said pettishly. "Why should I? It's not my nature. Besides, it's not the occupation of a gentleman."

Simon opened his eyes wide.

"But drawing is one of the best things in the world! I can't think how you can live in London and not want to draw! Everything is so beautiful and so interesting I could be drawing forever. And it is so useful; it helps you to remember what you have seen."

He glanced toward his own picture on the wall and Justin's eyes followed listlessly. Not much was visible from where they stood, but a face could be seen, and Justin said at once, "Why, that's Dido Twite."

"Do you know her?" Simon was a little surprised that a future duke should be acquainted with such a guttersnipe.

"Buckle, my tutor, used to lodge with her family and we called there once," Justin said indifferently. "I thought her a vilely impertinent brat."

"I lodge there now," Simon explained.

"Will you help me some more?" Justin said. "I expect old Fur-nose may come back soon."

The kitten had settled again, and Simon helped Justin with more sketches.

"Don't rely on how you think it ought to look," he repeated patiently, over and over. "Ask your eyes and make them tell your hand—look, his legs bend this way, not the way you have them—" and, as Justin rubbed out his line and obediently redrew it, he asked, "Why did your tutor leave the Twite house? Where is he living now?"

"With me, at Battersea Castle," Justin said, bored. "My uncle (he's my guardian; my parents are dead) he arranged it. I'd been doing lessons with Buckle in the mornings, but now he lives in and works as my uncle's steward too, and I have him on top of me all day long, prosing and preaching about my duty as a future duke, and I hate it, hate it, hate it!"

He jabbed his charcoal angrily at the paper and it snapped. Simon was disappointed. He had hoped the reason why Buckle left the Twite household might give him some clue as to Dr. Field's departure. He was about to put a further question when they heard voices outside. With a hasty gesture Justin waved him back to his corner behind the big jar and laid a finger on his lips. The door opened and Dr. Furneaux burst in briskly, whiskers waving.

"Eh bien, well, let us see how you have been getting on!" he demanded, bustling around the desk to look at Justin's drawings.

"Pas mal!" he declared. *"Pas mal du tout!"* You see—when you work wiss your head and do not merely s-scamp through ze drawing, all comes different! Ziss here, and ziss"—he poked at the sketches—"is a r-r-real artist's line. Here, not so good." Justin met his eyes nervously. "I am please wiss you, my boy, very please. Now I wish you to do some painting."

Justin turned pale at the idea, but Mr. Buckle, who had followed Dr. Furneaux into the room, interposed hastily, "I am afraid that won't be possible today, Dr. Furneaux. His Grace the Duke is expecting Lord Bakerloo to meet him at three on His Grace's barge to view the Chelsea Regatta."

"Barges—regattas," Dr. Furneaux grumbled, "a true painter does not sink of anysing but *painting! Eh bien,* be off, zen, if you muss, but bring me more drawings—more, more!—and better zan zese, next time you come."

Justin and Mr. Buckle nipped quickly out of the room almost before Dr. Furneaux had finished speaking. The little principal sat down at his desk, sighing heavily like a grampus.

Then the kitten, who had been investigating a dangling string of onions, managed to dislodge the whole lot and bring them crashing down onto himself. He bounded away, stiff-legged with fright. Simon burst out laughing.

"Tiens!" declared Dr. Furneaux. "It is ze doctor's boy. I had forgotten you, *mon gars. Voyons,* what have you been doing all zis time?"

Simon scrambled up, dusting charcoal from his knees, and Dr. Furneaux picked his way through the furniture until he could survey the whole drawing, which now occupied about seven square feet. Simon tried in vain to make out the doctor's reactions from his expression. Dr. Furneaux looked at the picture carefully for about five minutes without saying a word; sometimes he scrutinized some detail with his whiskers almost touching the charcoal, sometimes he stepped back as far as possible to observe the picture from a distance.

Simon had drawn several scenes, one in front of the other. In the foreground was Dido Twite, perched on the donkey, her pert sparrow's looks contrasting with its sleepy expression as she urged it along Rose Alley. To the right lay Mr. Cobb's yard, full of broken coaches, with the beaming Mr. Cobb leaning against a wheel, about to sip his mug of Organ-Grinder's Oil, and his men hard at work behind him.

"Wiss whom have you studied drawing before?" Dr. Furneaux asked sharply.

"With no one, sir. Dr. Field told me one or two things—that's all . . ."

Dr. Furneaux continued to study the picture and now rapped out a series of fierce questions—why had Simon placed this object there, that figure here, why had he drawn the man's leg like this, the steps thus, the donkey like that?

"I don't know, sir," Simon kept saying in bewilderment. "It seemed as if it ought to go that way."

He was beginning to be afraid that Dr. Furneaux must be angry when the little man amazed him by suddenly giving him a tremendous hug. Bristly whiskers nearly smothered him and the smell of garlic was overpowering.

"You are a good, good boy!" the doctor declared. "I am going to make a painter of you, but only if you work wiss every particle of yourself!"

"Yes, sir," Simon said faintly. All at once he felt excessively tired and hungry, his head ached, his arms and legs were stiff, he seemed to have been drawing in the stuffy room for half his lifetime.

"You will go now, you will come back tomorrow morning. Wiss you you will bring charcoal, brushes, oil paints—here, I give you ziss list—and palette. Zese sings you buy at one shop and at one shop only, zat is Bonnetiers in the King's Road."

"Yes, sir. How—how much will they cost?" Simon asked, doing feverish sums in his head, wondering how soon Mr. Cobb would pay him for his work, how much he would get, how late the paint shop stayed open.

Dr. Furneaux looked at him sharply and said, "For ziss time, you pay nossing. Here, I give you ziss note to Madame Bonnetier—"

"Oh, thank you-thank you, sir! And my fees? How much—"

"Never mind zat for ze moment. We shall see, later. Now, go, go! Do you sink ze pr-r-rincipal of ze academie has nossing to do but talk to you all day?" Dr. Furneaux plainly hated to be thanked. "Ah, bah, it is nossing, I too was once a poor ragged boy, *I!* Take ze little one, too."

He grabbed the kitten, which was on his desk again, and held it out. As he did so his eye fell on Justin's drawings. He checked a moment, his mouth opened, then shut. He stared at Simon as if about to ask something, then evidently changed his mind, sighed, and gestured him to go.

"He knew," Simon said to himself. "He knew I'd been helping Justin. I wonder if he was angry?"

3

When Simon returned to Rose Alley that evening it was late. He had been to the paint shop and bought beautiful new fat glistening tubes of paint, soft smooth brushes, and a glossy palette. Then he had returned to Mr. Cobb's yard where he was given about five jobs to do in quick succession—replacing a cracked panel in a barouche, mending a broken axletree, turning a new spoke and putting it in a chariot wheel, shoeing a pony, and bending an iron wheel tread. By the end of this grueling stint he was nearly dead of fatigue, and ravenous, but it was worth it, for Mr. Cobb, slapping him on the shoulder, pronounced him a prime all-arounder, paid him a guinea then and there, with the promise of as much work as he wanted, and invited him up for a dish of pigs' pettitoes and onions with Mrs. Cobb and young Miss Cobb, who lived in a little neat apartment up a flight of steps over the coach house at the back of the yard.

When he got home to Rose Alley he found Dido Twite swinging on the broken rails in front of the house.

"Why've you bin such a long time?" she greeted him.

"Working," said Simon.

"Watch me do a handstand. What you bin working at?"

"All sorts of things." He was very weary and disinclined for the company of this fidget of a child, but she seemed so delighted to see him that he lingered a minute or two, kindly admiring her antics.

"There's a circus coming to Southwark Friday week. D'you think they'd take me as a tumbler?"

"I'm not sure," Simon said cautiously. "Anyway you don't want to leave home, do you?"

"Don't I jist? Will you take me to the circus?"

"I may not be here still," said Simon, who had been offered lodgings at the Cobbs', and was inclined to move nearer to Rivière's Academy. Dido's face fell and she gazed at him open-mouthed. "Where can I get a wash?" he went on.

"Washus at the back," Dido said automatically. "Hot water's tuppence a bucket. Why won't you be here?"

"I may move to Chelsea. I'm going in now, good-by."

He ran whistling upstairs. From behind a closed door on the first floor came long, breathy, mournful notes. He heard Dido scurry up behind him and burst through the door crying, "Pa! *Pa!* Stop playing and listen."

Simon went on up to his own room, fed the kitten, and rummaged among the things in his pack for a small towel and a lump of soap he had made himself from wood ash and goose grease. Presently he ran downstairs again. As he neared the bottom a voice above him called, "Hey!"

He looked up and saw Dido hanging upside-down over the stair rail. She dropped a slice of bread-and-jam which landed jam-side downward on his head.

"Now look what you've done, you wretched brat!" said Simon crossly. He made a grab for her through the rail, but she retreated, screeching with laughter and mock alarm.

"Oo, you don't half look a sight! Jellyboy, jellyboy!"

"Just wait till I get you!" Simon threatened.

"What's it matter, you're going to wash anyway."

Simon reflected that this was true, and went out to the washhouse, which was in a lean-to at the back of the house. A fire burned under a large copper in a brick bunker; the water in the copper was steaming. In a corner behind a screen stood a tin bath, with a shower pan supported on iron legs above it. Simon poured hot water into the shower pan, undressed, and stepped into the bath. He pulled the string of the shower and hot water sluiced down on him and washed the jam out of his hair. He was soaping himself enjoyably when the washhouse door opened.

"Go away!" Simon shouted apprehensively. "I'm in the bath."

Dido's face came poking around the door. "It's only me,"she reassured him.

Simon scowled over the top of the screen. "Well, be off! It's not polite to come in when someone's bathing."

She skipped across the room. "Shall I take your clothes? You *would* look a nut-case then!"

"Don't you dare!"

"Well, will you give me a ride tomorrow?"

"All right."

She put his clothes down and retreated, turning in the doorway to say, "Pa says you're to come and have a dish of tea when you're ready."

Simon hurried out of the bath as soon as she had gone and put his clothes on again. While he was emptying the water in canfuls down a grated drain he heard voices apparently coming from the roof. This puzzled him until he realized that the chimney of the copper acted as a conductor for sound. What he could hear was the voices of Mr. and Mrs. Twite in their upstairs parlor.

". . . very annoying that he found his way here," Mrs. Twite was saying irritably.

Mr. Twite replied in a rumble of which nothing could be heard but the words "Dido . . . most unfortunate."

"Eustace says"—her voice came clearer, as if she had stepped toward the chimney piece—"best stay here under our eye for the time."

"I'm sure *I* don't care," her husband replied rather shrilly. "It's only *my* house after all. It's all one to me if Eustace and his ideas land us in the—"

"Quiet, Abednego! It's only for six weeks or so, in any case. Only till we can dispose of him by means of the dark dew. And you may be sure that we'll be handsomely rewarded when the Cause triumphs."

"Yes?" he said sourly. "We haven't had any reward for our other trouble yet, have we? I'm put upon, that's what it is, I'm put upon! All I want is to follow art and play my hoboy, but what happens?" He must have been walking across the room, for his words became fainter and Simon could hear nothing but a distant mumble in which the word "paint" was alone distinguishable.

He returned to his room with all his suspicions aroused once more. What—or who—was the cause of the "other trouble?" And was he himself the object of the Twites' conversation? And who was Eustace? And, even more mysterious, what was the dark dew by means of which somebody was to be disposed of? Poison? The Twites looked a shifty, havey-cavey lot, but he found it hard to believe they were poisoners.

The mournful music had begun again, but it stopped when he tapped at the Twites' door.

"Come in, come in, my dear young feller," boomed Mr. Twite, who in daylight proved to be a scraggy individual, thin and bony, with a wisp of hair and a wisp of beard and curiously wandering eyes that never stayed in one position very long. "Settling, are you?" he went on. "Capital, capital. All one happy family here, aren't we, Penny? Aren't we, Dido? Aren't we, Ella my dear?"

The young lady addressed as Penny replied listlessly, "Yes, Pa," and did not lift her eyes from a copy of *The Gentlewoman's Magazine* which she was studying. Dido, toasting bread at the fire, caught Simon's eye and pulled a face. Mrs. Twite, pouring hot water into a teapot, snapped, "Hold your hush, Abednego, and fetch the cordial."

Mr. Twite meekly laid down the large wooden instrument on which he had been playing (Simon guessed it to be his hoboy) and took a dusty black bottle out of a cupboard.

Mrs. Twite turned to Simon, all smiles. "Sit down, Mr. Thingummy, sit down, don't stand on ceremony here. (Dido—*move!*) You'll take a dish of tea, I hope?"

"Thank you, ma'am." Simon had already done very well at the Cobbs', but in order to be polite he accepted tea and toast.

"And a dash of mountain dew in it?" said Mr. Twite with the black bottle.

"No thank you," Simon said firmly. He wondered if this could be the dark dew, but decided it was not, after Mr. Twite had administered a large dram to himself and his lady, and a small one to Penelope. After a few sips of tea Mr. Twite, who had been looking rather gloomy, cheered up amazingly and began singing,

"Oh, it's dabbling in the dew that
makes the barmaids fair,
With their dewy, dewy eyes and their brassy, brassy hair!"

"Now, my dear boy," Mrs. Twite said to Simon, "We want to hear *all* about you."

"Yes," agreed Mr. Twite, putting down the dew bottle, "we want to hear *all* about you."

"*All* about you," murmured Penelope, without raising her eyes from the magazine, and even Dido piped up, *"All* about you," and dropped a fistful of toast crumbs down Simon's neck.

"Oh, there's not much to tell—" Simon began, but Mrs. Twite would have none of this.

"Dear boy, there must be. *Where* have you come from, *who* do you know, *what* are you going to do all day long in London?"

Question by question she drew from Simon all there was to know about him. At the age of three he had been found wandering in the village of Loose Chippings in Yorkshire. Nobody claimed him and, mysteriously, he could not speak a word of English, so he was sent to the Poor Farm, where unlucky orphans were starved and neglected by the overseer, Gloober, whose only interest was in the half crown per head per week he was paid by the parish. Here Simon survived as best he could for five years—he would not have endured it for so long, he said, had he not made a friend there whom he was reluctant to leave—until at the age of eight he decided to run away and live by himself in the woods.

"And that has been my life ever since," he concluded, "until last year I met Dr. Field and he said I should learn to paint, which I have long wanted to do."

"But what a *romantic* tale!" exclaimed Mrs. Twite, casting her eyes up. "Is it not, Abednego? And did you never hear what happened to your friend?"

"Oh, she's in London too," Simon said happily. "I had the good luck to see her today. But about Dr. Field—I wrote to him, to this address, saying when I should arrive. Was my letter not delivered here?"

"Never, dear boy."

"And Dr. Field has not been here?"

"Neither hide nor hair of him," declared Mr. Twite.

"Now is not that a curious thing? But of course there are many, *many* Rose Alleys in London and I daresay we shall find that your Dr. Field is living at one of the *others* and, when you discover which one, why then you will be happily reunited. Depend upon it, that is the explanation, do you not agree, my dove?"

"Oh, undoubtedly," agreed Mrs. Twite. "But in the meantime, my dear Mr. Thingummy, you mustn't *think* of moving away. We've begun to look on you as one of us, haven't we, girls?"

"Yes," yawned Penelope, bored, looking at a picture of a lady's dolman with bugled ruching.

"Besides, if you moved away and Dr. Field *should* chance to make his way here, think what a misfortune if you missed one another!"

"Then you are expecting him?" Simon said hopefully.

"Never heard of him till today, dear boy. But if *you* are looking for *him,* it stands to reason that *he* must be looking for *you,* doesn't it?"

"I suppose so," Simon said doubtfully. He glanced about, half hoping for some trace of Dr. Field's presence. The room was large and extremely shabby; it contained several down-at-bottom armchairs, a table covered with dingy red plush, a potted palm in a brass pot, and a piano with several of its yellowed keys missing.

"You play?" said Mr. Twite, following the direction of Simon's eyes to the piano. "You are a follower of Terpsycore?

"No," said Simon, without the least notion as to who

Terpsy-core could be.

"All my family sing and play. My dear wife, the triangle. My sister-in-law, the violoncello. Dido, the hoboy like myself. Penelope and my father-in-law, the pianoforte. Penelope my dear, you shall play and sing for us, to welcome our young friend into our circle."

"No I shan't, Pa," said Penelope shortly, and returned to her reading. Simon thought her a disagreeable girl. She was pale and, like Dido, had straw-colored hair which was elaborately dressed in ringlets. She wore a showy gown adorned with floss and spangles. She caught Simon's eye, gave him a scornful glance, yawned again, and said, "Isn't anyone coming in tonight?"

Simon excused himself, explaining that he had to be up early.

"Now you won't *think* of moving, dear boy, will you?" Mrs. Twite gave him a toothy smile. "We might even—*even*—see our way to lowering your rent." She thought this over and added, "Washing water reduced to three halfpence a bucket."

"Thank you." Simon wondered why the Twites, last night not at all keen to have a lodger, were now so anxious to persuade him to stay.

He was at the door, about to say good night, when it opened smartly in his face and a woman walked in carrying a cello. She was looking behind her as she walked, and she called to somebody behind her, "Put them in the kitchen, Tod, do; mind you don't drop the cabbages." She turned to Mrs. Twite and added, "There's cabbages, Ella, and as nice a basket of potatoes as you'll find this side of the Garden."

"Thank you, Tinty," Mrs. Twite said, looking a little flustered. "This is our new lodger, Mr. Thingummy. My sister Mrs. Grotch."

"Good evening," Simon said. Mrs. Grotch, too, appeared disconcerted, but nodded stiffly. On his way up to bed Simon glanced down the stairs and saw the boy, Tod, stagger into the Twites' kitchen with a heavy load of mixed vegetables. Simon's suspicions were confirmed. For Tod was the boy who had snatched his letter on Southwark Bridge and Mrs. Grotch, or Aunt Tinty, was the little woman who had misdirected him. A slow plodding step was now audible coming up the stairs from the front door. Simon lingered, waiting to see if his last guess was right, and was rewarded. For the old man who came into view, pulling himself up laboriously by the handrail and pausing to take a long quavering breath on each step was the same white-bearded elder whom he had last seen on Southwark Bridge talking about his youth in the forest of Epping.

4

When Simon woke next day he heard the rain beating against his window. He opened the casement and a wild gust of wind surged about the room, so he shut it again hastily. As on the previous day, when he went downstairs, the Twite family seemed wrapped in slumber. However his arrival at the front door coincided with the postman's knock, and a cascade of letters shot through the slot. Miss Penelope Twite instantly darted out of a nearby door, snatched up the letters, yawning, and gave Simon a hostile glance. She was wearing a faded gingham wrapper, her hair was in curlpapers, and she seemed in a very irritable humor. As she retired again Simon heard her say snappishly, "You can do it tomorrow morning—" then there was a stifled grunt and a creak of springs as if someone had jumped back into bed, slamming the door behind them.

Simon went out wondering if the Twites had a particular reason for not wanting him to see the mail. In case there might be a letter for Dr. Field? However, as soon as he stepped outside he was obliged to direct all his energy to keeping himself upright and the kitten dry in the wild gusts of wind and rain that seemed threatening to knock him off his feet. He was glad that it was not far to the academy, and thankful to gain the shelter of its great portico. Here he was approached by the young man whom he had seen yesterday washing socks.

"Hallo, my cocky," said this individual. "Old Fur-nose told me to watch out for you. So here's poor old Gus, eyes like cannonballs from lack of sleep, hoisted from the downy before the Chelsea cocks have left their watery nests—particular watery this morning, wasn't it, Fothers? Ugh!" he added, shuddering. "*Eight o'clock!* To think such a time exists! There ought to be a law against it, so there should!"

"I'm sorry if I've kept you waiting, sir," Simon apologized.

"We've only just this minute got here," interposed the young man with him whom he addressed as Fothers. "We've orders to take you to the Mausoleum, but I daresay you could do with a cup of coffee first?"

"Here, young 'un, just hold that bit of tinder, will you?" Gus pulled out flint and steel and a handful of carpenters' shavings from his pouch and soon expeditiously kindled a small fire under the shelter of the portico.

Meanwhile Fothers had run down to the river shore—only a stone's throw from the academy—and returned with an armful of driftwood and tarry splinters, damp, to be sure, but ready to blaze up with a little encouragement. In no time a handsome fire was burning, over which Fothers dexterously slung a tin paint-pot full of water. "No cooking at our lodgings," he explained, tossing in a handful of coffee, "ever since Gus started a fire and nearly burnt the landlady in her bed. So we have breakfast here."

"Pity I didn't succeed in frizzling the old skinflint," Gus remarked morosely, dropping three eggs into the coffeepot. "Seven minutes for mine, Fothers, I fancy 'em hard. Hey, you, What's-your-name, have you any bread on you?"

"Yes, sir." Simon had purchased a long loaf and a sausage on the way to Chelsea. He was delighted to contribute to the meal.

"Ah, that's good, devilish good," exclaimed Gus, his eyes lighting up. "I haven't had my grinders in a bit of solid prog for three days; had just about enough of nibbling old Mrs. Grobb's parsley and spring onions from her window boxes. But you mustn't call us Sir, young 'un, we're only poor students, same as yourself. This is Democracy Hall, this is."

While he waited for his egg to boil he pulled a cake of soap from his pocket, held it out in the rain a moment, rubbed up a lather on his jaw, and then, with a palette knife which he drew from his painter's satchel, proceeded calmly to shave, using the lid of the coffee tin as a mirror. By the time he had done, Fothers, who had been timing the eggs with a large turnip watch, pronounced them ready.

Simon, who was wet and chilled, found himself very glad of the drink of hot coffee. He noticed that his new friends, though they were plainly very hungry, showed great delicacy in eating only sparingly of his bread and sausage. He pressed more on them.

"No, thank'ee, young 'un" said Fotheringham. "You'll be wanting it yourself come dinnertime. Sausages don't grow on trees in London, you know, and they aren't giving away any half crowns yet, that I've heard. Come along, now, and I'll show you the way to the Mausoleum."

This proved to be an enormous room containing a regular forest of statues: sitting, standing, lying, in marble, metal, and granite, they seemed as if they had sprouted from the floor like mustard-and-cress.

"Old Fur-nose always makes you start by drawing these," Gus explained.

"*All* of them?" Simon looked round in alarm.

"Bless you, no! Depends if he likes you—then he moves you on quick enough. *You'll* be all right—anyone could tell he'd taken quite a shine to you."

"Thank you!" Simon called after them as they left. Presently Dr. Furneaux came bustling in, directed Simon to draw a statue of a lady who appeared to be wearing nothing but a fish net, uttered words of instruction and encouragement in his ear, and then surged around the room, praising, scolding, and exhorting the other students.

The day passed quickly. As usual when Simon drew he hardly noticed the passage of time. The kitten foraged among the statues and received a share of bread and sausage at dinnertime. At last the light began to fade, and Simon rubbed his stiff hand.

"Enough, enough, now, boy," exclaimed Dr. Furneaux, materializing beside him like a whiskery ghost in the dusk.

"Ze ozzers zey all pack up and finish long ago. To draw in ze dark is to r-rruin ze eyes. Away wiss you and come back *matinalement,* in good time, tomorrow morning."

He peered at Simon's drawing, said, "Good boy," and bustled away. Simon went off to Mr. Cobb's yard where he worked hard at splicing shafts for a couple of hours. Mr. Cobb himself was in the smithy, superintending the shoeing of an excitable little bay mare. Presently he came out, rubbing the sweat off his brow.

"Proper handful she be," he said with a grin. "Artful as a curricle-load o' monkeys. She come in a-hobbling from her cast shoe, and now she've lamed the young feller as brought her—kicked him on the kneecap and he's limping like a tinker's moke. He allus was an unhandy chap, was my wife's cousin Jem."

Another explosion of whinnies came from the forge. The little mare danced out, making circles around the smith, who was leading her. Another man followed, limping and cursing.

"Here, Jem, boy, you'd best goo up to Floss. Ask her to rub some liniment on that knee," Mr. Cobb said. "Knee like that goes proud on you, you'll be lame for months. I dessay his Grace the Dook 'on't mind waiting for the mare."

"'Tain't his Grace," Jem said sulkily. "It's for my young Lord Whippersnapper. Nothing would please his fancy but he must go riding by torchlight in the park, and no other mount in the stable but this one would do for him to set his lordly seat on. Dang me, was there ever such a pother when 'twas found she'd a shoe loose! Nowt would serve but I must take and have her shod this instant. And he's waiting for her now." He moved to take the mare's bridle, limped again heavily, and let out an involuntary groan.

"You bide here along, Jem, boy," said Mr. Cobb concernedly. "One o' the others can take the filly back."

"I'll go!" said Simon instantly, putting a finished shaft with a pile of others. "Where shall I take her?"

"Ah, that's me boy! 'Twon't take you but a minute. Only a step from here it be. Duke o' Battersea's stables. Goo in the back way, through the tunnel, ask for Mr. Waters, he's the head groom, give him my compliments, and say my Floss is putting a tar poultice on Jem's knee and he'll be right as rain before Goose-Friday."

"Is the boy trustworthy?" Jem asked, shooting a doubtful glance at Simon. "He won't take the filly over to Smithfield and sell her for cat's meat?"

"Trustworthy as my old mother," said Mr. Cobb heartily. "Come on now, Jem, boy, what you need is a drop of Organ-Grinder's Oil." He helped the limping Jem up the stairs, shouting for Flossie to get out the tar and a large saucepan.

Simon tucked the kitten into his jacket, took the mare's bridle from the smith, and led her out of the gate and along the riverbank to Chelsea Bridge. Beyond, across the river, was the noble pile of Battersea Castle.

Gus had pointed out the castle that morning while they were breakfasting; Simon had been delighted to learn that the place where his friend Sophie lived was so near, and had been planning to go to the servants' entrance as soon as possible and ask to see her. Returning the mare offered an excellent opportunity and he had seized it at once.

He paused a moment, gazing in awe at the huge mass of buildings composing the castle. It stood close to the river; on either side and to the rear stretched the extensive park and gardens, filled with splendid trees, fountains, and beds of brilliant flowers in shades of pink, crimson, or scarlet. The castle itself was built of pink granite, and enclosed completely a smaller, older building which the present Duke's father had considered too insignificant for his town residence. The new castle had taken forty years to build; three architects and hundreds of men had worked day and night, and the old Duke had personally selected every block of sunset-colored stone that went to its construction. "I want it to look like a great half-open rose," he declared to the architects, who were fired with enthusiasm by this romantic fancy. It was begun as a wedding present to the Duke's wife, whose name was Rosamond, but unfortunately she died some nine years before it was completed. "Never mind, it will do for her memorial instead," said the grief-stricken but practical widower. The work went on. At last the final block was laid in place. The Duke, by now very old, went out in his barouche and drove slowly along the opposite riverbank to consider the effect. He paused midway for a long time, then gave his opinion. "It looks like a cod cutlet covered in shrimp sauce," he said, drove home, took to his bed, and died. But his son, the fifth and present Duke, who had been born and brought up in the castle, lived in it contentedly enough, and was only heard to utter one complaint about it. "It's too dry," he said. "Not enough mildew." For the fifth Duke was a keen natural scientist, and molds were one of his passions.

At this time of day the great pink structure was lit by a circle of blazing gas flambeaux which vied with the smoky rose-color of the London sunset and were reflected in the river below.

Glancing about him, Simon noticed a sign at the foot of the bridge: *Battersea Castle. Tradesmen and Servants Turn Left*. Obediently he turned, and found the entrance to a large tunnel which ran under the river. The mare went forward confidently into it with ears pricked; plainly she knew her way home and was not startled by the booming echoes which her hoofbeats called out from the curving walls. The tunnel was not dark, for gas lamps hung at regular intervals from the roof, but it was rather damp; rain from the morning's storm had collected on the floor in large pools. Toward the middle one of these extended for some twenty feet.

Simon, leading the mare, splashed unconcernedly through; having lived in the woods for years he was not worried by a trifle like wet feet. But he saw a girl some way ahead of him pause at the edge of the large puddle; then a man, who had been walking some paces behind her, overtook her and picked her up to carry her through. When the man was well into the middle of the pool, however, he evidently began to tickle the girl, for she screamed and struggled. Simon, approaching, heard him say, "You'd best promise to come with me to the bear-baiting on Saturday or I'll drop you in. One . . . two . . . three . . ."

"I'll do no such thing!" exclaimed the girl with spirit. "You know I can't abide the bear-baiting."

"Then I'll drop you."

"Oh!" exclaimed the girl furiously. *"How* I'd box your ears if my hands weren't full of grapes and thistles. Will you stop being so provoking and let me get on! My lady's waiting for these things."

"I shan't budge till you promise."

Neither of the pair had noticed Simon: their voices had covered the sound of the mare's hoofs. He recognized the girl as Sophie and was about to come to her aid when there was an unexpected interruption.

A painter's cradle had been slung from the roof, and an elderly man who had been lying on it, attentively regarding the stonework, suddenly loosed a rope, letting himself down with a rattle of pulleys, until he dangled in front of the disputing couple.

"Midwink!" he barked, "Leave the girl alone!"

The man was so startled that he almost dropped Sophie.

"Y-y-yes, of course, sir!" he gulped.

"Put her down! No, not there, dolt—" for Midwink made as if to deposit Sophie in the pool, "take her along to the dry road."

"Certainly, certainly, sir."

"And don't let me see you up to such tricks again, or you'll go back to Chippings and stay there."

"Oh, no, sir! Please don't send me back there, please!"

"Well, behave yourself!" said the man on the cradle

severely, and he hauled on the pulley and shot up to the roof again, muttering, "Where had I got to? Aha, what have we here? Something of definite mycological interest, I feel positive."

The man Midwink carried Sophie across the pool and put her down. Then he noticed Simon and gave him a malevolent look. He was a hatchet-faced individual, dressed in black plush with buckled shoes and a stiff white collar. There was something mean, shifty, and bad-tempered about his appearance; he looked as if he would be a nasty customer to cross.

"Who might *you* be?" he said, eyeing Simon up and down, at the same moment as Sophie cried out in joyful recognition, "*Simon!* It's Simon! How in the world did you get here?"

"I've brought the bay mare from Mr. Cobb," Simon said.

"Horseflesh is not my province," Midwink remarked loftily. "You'd best take the mare to the stables."

"I'll show you the way," Sophie said. "I'm going there myself. But Simon, how amazing it is that you should be in London. *Oh,* I am so pleased! I was beginning to fear we should never see each other again."

"I see you've found a *friend,* Miss Fine-Airs," sneered Midwink. "Nice sort of riffraff you slight decent folk for, I must say! What would her Grace think if she saw you consorting with horse-yobs and gutter-boys—there wouldn't be so much of 'my pretty Sophie' then!"

"Oh, be quiet, Midwink—I do not find you interesting at all!" snapped Sophie.

Simon chuckled quietly to himself. Sophie's speech was so very characteristic that he wondered how he could have forgotten it. She had a trick of rattling out her words very fast and clearly, like a handful of beads dropped on a plate. He wondered where he had recently heard somebody else speak in the same way.

"*I* know when I'm not wanted," said Midwink sourly, "But you'd best guard your tongue, Madam Sophie—a pretty face isn't the only passport to fortune here, as you may find!"

"Who's he?" asked Simon, as Midwink walked ahead of them and took a turning to the right.

"Oh, he is the duke's valet—he is of no account," Sophie said impatiently. "He would be turned off it it were not for his knack of tying cravats. The duke has grown too shortsighted to tie his own, and Midwink is the only person who can arrange them to his liking. But tell me, how do you come to be in London? Did you ever go back to Gloober's Poor Farm? What have you been doing all these years? Oh, there is so *much* to ask you! But I must run to my lady with these things—she is waiting to embroider them. Can we meet tomorrow—it is my evening off, are you free then? Ah, that is good, excellent, I will meet you, where? Not too near the castle or Midwink may come bothering—Cobb's Yard? Yes indeed I know it, that will do very well. Now, here are the stables and there is Mr. Waters. Good evening, Mr. Waters, here is my friend Simon who has brought back your horse."

"That ain't no horse, Miss Sophie, that's as neat a little

filly as yourself," said Mr. Waters.

"Ah, bah, horses and fillies are all the same to me! Simon, it is *wonderful* to see you again. Now I must fly. Till tomorrow!" She stood on tiptoe to give Simon a quick peck on the cheek, then ran off with her basket.

"And where's Jem Suds got to?" asked Mr. Waters. ("Come up, my beauty, then, hold still while I put a saddle on your pernickety back.")

Simon explained about the kicked knee and Mrs. Cobb's tar poultice.

"That lad's born to get his neck broke," sighed Mr. Waters, tightening a girth. "Ah, there's his young lordship, you just brought the mare back in time—"

"Aren't you ready yet, Waters?" called an irritable voice, and a boy came out of a doorway. Simon recognized Justin, the unwilling art student. He swung himself rather clumsily into the saddle, then looked down at Simon. "Oh, hallo," he said carelessly. "What are you doing here?" He did not, however, wait for an answer, but gave a flip with his crop and trotted across the stable yard and out through a gateway that led into the park.

"Wait, your lordship!" called Waters. "I've got Firefly saddled, I'll be with you directly." He led out another mount, but Justin impatiently called back, "I don't want you, Waters, I want to be on my own," set spurs to the mare, and galloped off into the dusk.

"Pesky young brat!" growled Waters. "He knows he's not allowed out alone. Now I suppose I shall have to chase him all over the park, afore he breaks his neck."

"Who was that?" Simon asked.

"Young Lord Bakerloo, the Dook's nevvy. He's the hair, as his Grace never had none o' his own . . . Good-by, my lad, thank you for bringing back the filly," Waters called as he rode out of the gate.

Simon made his way back through the tunnel.

The elderly gentleman was still slung up on his painter's cradle halfway along, gazing at the roof through a magnifying glass. Simon had forgotten about him, and was rather startled at being addressed by a voice above his head as he waded through the largest puddle.

"It's rather damp down there, isn't it?"

"It *is* rather damp," Simon agreed, pausing and looking up politely.

"You find it inconvenient?" the old man asked, betraying a certain anxiety.

"Bless you, no!" Simon said cheerfully.

The man brightened up at once.

"You don't mind a bit of damp? You're a boy after my own heart! *I* don't mind damp either. In fact I *like* damp. You don't find it troublesome? That's excellent—excellent."

"I suppose it's a bit of a nuisance for females," Simon suggested, thinking of Sophie's white cambric skirts. The man's face fell.

"For females? You think it is? Yes, perhaps—perhaps." He sighed. "Still, you yourself don't object to it—that's very gratifying. It's always gratifying to find a kindred spirit. Do you, I wonder, play chess?"

"Yes I do, sir," said Simon, who had been taught to play by Dr. Field.

"You do? But that's capital—famous!" The old gentleman looked radiant. "We must certainly meet again. You must come and play chess with me. Will you?"

"Why, certainly, sir," said Simon, who began to believe the old gentleman must be a trifle cracked. Still, he seemed a harmless old boy, and quite kindly disposed. "When shall I come?"

"Let me think. Not tomorrow night, dinner with the Prince of Wales. Night after, Royal Society, lecture on moss. Night after that, tennis with the Archbishop. (Indoor, of course.) Night after, Almack's with Henrietta. (Devilish dull, but she enjoys it.) Night after, ball at Carlton House. Stuffy affairs, can't be helped, must put in an appearance. Night after, billiards with the Lord Chief Justice. How about today week?"

"That would be quite all right for me, sir," said Simon. "Where shall I come?"

"Oh, I'm always around and about," the man said, waving a hand vaguely. "Anyone will tell you where to find me. Any time after nine. That's excellent—really delightful." He pulled on a rope and his cradle moved away.

"Excuse me sir—whom shall I ask for?" Simon called after him.

"Just ask for Battersea," the man's voice came faintly back.

Battersea? Battersea? He *must* be cracked, Simon decided. No doubt by that day week he would have forgotten all about the invitation. Perhaps Sophie would know who he was, and whether the invitation should be taken seriously or not. Sophie was so shrewd and cheerful and kindhearted—what a comfort it was to have found her again!

Leaving the tunnel, Simon swung on toward Vauxhall Bridge, whistling happily. If only he could find Dr. Field, life in London would not be so bad!

5

Next day, chancing to wake early, Simon looked out of his front window into Rose Alley and saw his unfortunate donkey, Caroline, struggling to pull an outrageously heavy milk cart loaded with churns, and being encouraged thereto by the shrewish dairywoman, who was beating her with a curtain pole.

Simon threw on his clothes and ran down to the street.

"Hey!" he shouted after the milkwoman. She turned, scowling, and snapped, "Penny a gill, and only if you've got your own jug."

"I don't want milk," Simon said (indeed it looked very blue and watery). "I want my donkey." And before she could object, he kicked a brick under the wheel of the cart and slipped the relieved Caroline out from between the shafts. In two days she seemed to have grown noticeably thinner and to have acquired several weals.

"I'm not leaving her with you a minute longer," Simon told the woman. "You ought to be ashamed to treat her so."

"I suppose you are the president of the Royal Humane

Society," she sneered. Then she turned and bawled, "Tod! Bring the mule."

"Coming, Aunt Poke," called a voice, and the boy Tod appeared leading a scraggy mule with one hand and holding his trousers around his neck with the other. He put out his tongue at Simon, and remarked, "What price cat's meat?"

It was still very early, and Simon decided this would be a good time to make inquiries about Dr. Field at the shops in the neighborhood. There was a greengrocer's next to the dairy, adorned with piles of wizened radishes and bunches of drooping parsley. He saw Mrs. Grotch, Aunt Tinty, watering these with dirty water from a battered can. Guessing that he would get no help from her he passed to the next shop, a bakery.

"Can you tell me if a Dr. Gabriel Field ever bought bread here?" he asked, stepping into the warm, sweet-smelling place.

"Dr. Field?" The baker scratched his head, then called to his wife, "Polly? Know anything about a Dr. Field?"

"Was he the one that lanced Susie's carbuncle?" The baker's wife came through into the shop, wiping her hands on her apron.

Just at that moment Simon heard a voice behind him. Tod, having harnessed the mule to his Aunt Poke's milk float, had wandered along the lane and was spinning a top outside the door and singing in a loud, shrill voice,

"Nimmy, nimmy, not,
My name's Tom Tit Tot."

Whether this song had any effect on the baker and his wife, or whether they had just recollected a piece of urgent business, Simon could not be sure, but the baker said hastily, "No, there's no doctor of that name round here, young man," and hurried out of the shop, while his wife cried, "Mercy! my rolls are burning," and bustled after him.

Simon walked the length of the row of shops, asking at each one, but all his questions, perhaps because of Tod, were equally fruitless, and at length, discouraged, he set off for the academy, while Tod turned a series of cartwheels along Rose Alley (keeping his trousers on only with the greatest difficulty) and launched a defiant shout of "My name's Tom Tit Tot" after Simon which it seemed wisest to ignore.

It was still only half-past seven, so there was time to call at the Cobbs' and ask if Caroline might be boarded at the stables there.

The Cobbs were at breakfast and received Simon with great cordiality, offering him marmalade pie, cold fowl, and hot boiled ham. Mrs. Cobb, a stout, motherly woman, insisted on his having a mug of her Breakfast Special to see him through the day. This was a nourishing mixture of hot milk and spices, tasting indeed so powerfully of aniseed that Simon thought it would see him through not only that day but several days to come.

"Ah, it's a reg'lar cockle-warmer, Flossie's Breakfast Special," Mr. Cobb said fondly and proudly. "You see, young 'un, my wife was a Fidgett, from Loose Chippings;

those Fidgett girls know more about housewifery and the domestic arts by the time they marry than most women learn in a lifetime."

Simon was very interested to hear that Mrs. Cobb came from the same part of the country as himself, while Mrs. Cobb was amazed to learn that Simon had passed the early part of his life at Gloober's Poor Farm.

"And you such a stout, sensible lad, too!" she exclaimed. "I thought they all turned out half-starved and wanting in the head, poor things. O' course we'll keep the donkey here, and gladly, won't we, Cobby! The lad won't mind if little Libby has a turnout on her now and then, I daresay?"

As little Libby Cobb was only two, and looked extremely seraphic, in complete contrast to Miss Dido Twite, Simon had not the least objection to this.

He bade farewell to the Cobbs, hastened down to the academy, and set to work in the Mausoleum, drawing a bronze figure with a trident. He had not, however, been at this occupation very long when Dr. Furneaux appeared and whisked him away to another room where an old lavender-seller had been established with her baskets on a platform to have her portrait painted by a dozen students.

They had been working for a couple of hours and Dr. Furneaux was giving a lecture from the platform (largely incomprehensible because he had somehow got his whiskers smothered in charcoal dust and kept breaking off to sneeze) when two people entered the room.

Glancing around his easel Simon recognized the boy Justin, whom he now knew to be young Lord Bakerloo, the

Duke of Battersea's nephew, and his tutor, the pale-eyed Mr. Buckle. Justin looked wan but triumphant; his right arm was heavily bandaged and he carried it in a sling.

Buckle addressed Dr. Furneaux in low tones. Meanwhile Justin had caught sight of Simon and nodded to him familiarly.

"Brought it off!" he confided, gesturing with his bandaged arm (which appeared to give him no great pain). "Done old Fur-nose brown, I have. Can't paint with my dib-dabs in a clout, can I?"

"Did you take a toss?" Simon asked, remembering the headlong way Justin had galloped across the twilit park.

"Walk*er!*" Justin replied, laying the first finger of his left hand alongside his nose. "That'd be telling."

"Yes indeed, *most* regrettable," Mr. Buckle was saying sorrowfully to Dr. Furneaux. "But we must be thankful the accident was no worse. The doctor fears Lord Bakerloo will not be able to use his right hand for at least a month."

"My dear Justin—my poor Justin!" Dr. Furneaux exclaimed warmly, darting to Justin, who winced away nervously. "Ziss is most tragic news! A painter has no business wiss riding on a horse—it is by far too dangerous."

"I'm not a painter, I'm a Duke's grandson," Justin muttered, but he concealed from Dr. Furneaux his look of satisfaction at being told not to return until his arm was completely healed.

When evening came and the students departed to their homes, Simon returned to Mr. Cobb's yard, where he was to meet Sophie, and occupied the interval by blacksmith's work. He had just finished bending an iron rim onto a wheel when she arrived.

"Why!" cried Mr. Cobb. "Is *this* your friend? It's the bonny lass as waits on her Grace. Dang me, but you're a lucky young fellow!"

Sophie had brought a basket of fruit and proposed that she and Simon should walk into Battersea Park and eat their supper sitting on the grass. But the hospitable Mr. Cobb would not hear of such a plan.

"Look at the sky!" he admonished them. "Full to busting! There's enough rain up there for a week of Sundays. You'll just be a-setting down to your first nibble when it comes peltering down on you. No, no, you come upstairs and eat your dinners comfor'ble under a roof; Flossie would never let me hear the last of it if I let two young 'uns go off to catch their deaths of pewmony."

Sophie protested that it was putting the Cobbs to a deal too much trouble but as the sky was indeed very threatening they finally accepted, and in return offered to mind Miss Libby Cobb while her mother slipped around the corner to buy two pounds of Best Fresh and a gallon jar of pickled onions.

Young Miss Cobb proved remarkably easy to amuse; she and the kitten chased one another till both were exhausted, and when that happened Simon or Sophie had only to imitate the noise of some animal to put her in fits of laughter. Meanwhile Sophie told Simon all that had happened to her since Simon had run away from Gloober's Poor Farm.

"I was lucky," she said. "You remember I always liked

needlework and Mrs. Gloober used to get me to do her mending? Then she began buying fashion magazines and bringing them home for me to make up her dresses. One time I was at work on a blue *peau de chameau* ball dress with Vandykes of lace and plush roses when her Grace the Duchess came in to inspect the Poor Farm and saw the dress. Next day a pony trap came over from Chippings Castle: the Duchess's compliments and she'd take the little girl who was so clever with her needle to be a sewing maid. Mrs. Gloober was very angry but she didn't dare refuse because the Duchess was on the Board. But she packed me off without a thing to wear. Since then her Grace has been *so* kind to me, and now I'm her lady's maid; when their Graces came up to London for the summer I came with them."

Then Simon in turn told his story, finishing with the mysterious disappearance of Dr. Field and the odd and suspicious behavior of the Twite family.

Meanwhile Miss Libby Cobb had again started in pursuit of the kitten. At this moment she caught her foot in a thick rag rug, the pride of Mrs. Cobb's heart, tripped, and fell against the door opening onto the stairhead. Not firmly latched, it flew open, and there was a thump and a shout. Sophie sprang to catch Libby before she could tumble downstairs, and exclaimed, "Why, it's Jem! What ever are you doing there, Jem?"

Jem indeed it was, but in no condition to answer. He must have been just outside the door when Libby fell against it, and the unexpected push had sent him down the stairs. He lay groaning at the bottom.

"We'd best get the poor fellow up here," Simon proposed, but before they could do so Mrs. Cobb returned from her shopping and let out a shriek of dismay.

"Eh, Jem my man, never tell me you're in the wars again, just when I'd set you right with a tar poultice! What happened?" she asked, as she and Simon between them supported the unlucky Jem up the stairs.

"The door flew open and knocked me down," he muttered.

"And what was you doing then—listening at the keyhold?" Jem turned pale. "Nay, only my joke, lad, never heed it. I do believe all the ill-luck in Battersea falls on your poor head. Come you in and lie down on Libby's bed while I put a bit o' vinegar on it."

While Mrs. Cobb ministered to the afflicted Jem, Sophie flew about very capably and set to cooking the Best Fresh, and Simon made a monstrous heap of toast and extracted the stopper of the pickled-onion jar. Soon they sat down to a very cheerful meal with the Cobbs.

Sophie and Mrs. Cobb had a fine time exchanging gossip, for Mrs. Cobb, it appeared, had been a parlormaid at Chippings Castle before she got married.

"Ah, you're in clover working for her Grace," she declared. "As sweet a lady you'll not find this side of Ticklepenny Corner, poor thing. It's a shame she never had no little ones of her own; if she'd 'a had, I'll be bound they'd be worth twenty of that puny little whey-faced lad they call Lord Bakerloo. He's the Duke's nevvy, you see," she went on (like all old retainers, she loved talking about the Family). "The Duke's younger brother, Henry, he married his own cousin, and they had Justin, that was born abroad in Hanoverian parts and sent back to England as a babby when both his parents died. Deary dear, it was a sad end, poor young things, and a sad beginning too—there was aplenty trouble when they married."

"Why?" asked Sophie.

"Because they were cousins, and she was half French, and a wild one! Her ma was Lady Helen Bayswater, that's the present Duke's aunt—she fell in love with a French painter escaped from France in the revolution they had, and married him in the teeth of her family as you might say. Famous, he was, but not grand family."

"Was his name Marius Rivière?" asked Simon.

"That's it! I never can get my tongue round those Frenchy names! He married Lady Helen and they had the one daughter—what was *her* name? It'll come to me in a minute—and for some time they was at daggers drawn with the old Duke. They say Rivière had been great friends with all the family before, and painted pictures of 'em, but the marriage broke it up. Then Lady Helen's daughter met her cousin, his present Grace's younger brother, and they fell in love, and the trouble began all over. They ran off to Hanover, where his regiment was, and got married. And that was the last that was heard, till word was sent they was dead, and Mr. Buckle fetched back the poor babby. By that the old Duke was dead, and his present Grace had always been fond of his brother, and stood by him, so he brought up Justin."

"It's rather sad," Sophie said. "Poor Justin. You can understand why he always seems so miserable. Specially if he has been looked after by that sour Mr. Buckle all his life."

"Do you know," exclaimed Mrs. Cobb, who had been scrutinizing Simon and Sophie as they sat side by side in the window seat, "you two are as alike as two chicks in a nest! I declare, you might be brother and sister. Are you related?"

They stared at one another in astonishment. Such an idea had never occurred to them. How strange it would be if they were!

"We don't know, ma'am," Sophie said at length. "We came to the Poor Farm at different times, you see. I was brought up by a kind old man, a charcoal burner in the forest, till I was seven, and then the parish overseer came and took me away and said I must be with the other orphans. But the old man was not my father, I know. I can remember when he first found me."

"Who looked after you before that, then, child?"

"An otter in the forest," Sophie explained. "I can still recall how difficult it was to learn human language, and how strange it seemed to eat anything but fish."

"An *otter!* Merciful gracious!" Mrs. Cobb flung up her hands. "An otter and then a charcoal burner! It's a wonder you grew up such a beauty, my dear! I'd 'a thought you'd have had webbed feet at the very least!"

"They were both very kind to me," Sophie said, laughing. "I was dreadfully sad when the overseer came and took me to Gloober's."

"I don't wonder, my dear, from what I've heard of the place."

"If Simon hadn't taken care of me there I don't know how I'd have got on for the first few years. Later it wasn't so bad, when I learned dressmaking, and Mrs. Gloober found I could be useful to her."

"But you like it better with her Grace?"

"Oh yes, a thousand times! Her Grace is so kind! Sometimes she seems more like an aunt or a godmother than a mistress! Mercy!" Sophie suddenly cried, jumping up as the solemn notes of the Chelsea Church clock boomed out the hour. "Ten o'clock already! It's time I was getting back to make her Grace's hot posset. She always likes it soon after ten."

"I'll see you home," Simon said. They bade good-by to the kindly Cobbs, who invited them to come again whenever they had an hour to spare. Halfway down the stairs they were halted by a hoarse shout from above, and turned to see Jem looking through the bedroom doorway, his hair all in spikes and his eyes staring with sleep.

"Soph . . . please . . . " he mumbled. "Could . . . give . . . note . . . Mr. Buckle?" He thrust a piece of crumpled paper into Sophie's hand.

"He's half asleep. It's the poppy syrup I gave him," said Mrs. Cobb concernedly, and steered him back to bed.

"I'll deliver your note!" Sophie called, but Jem was already unconscious again. Sophie tried to straighten out the paper, which appeared to be a sugar bag. The large sprawling script on it covered both sides:

> MISTER BUKKLE. SUM ONE CUMS FROM U NO WHERE. JEM.

"Oh dear," Sophie said, "Now I've read it, but I didn't mean to. In any case I haven't the least notion what it means. I hope Mr. Buckle will understand it."

"By the way," Simon said, "I had a queer invitation after I saw you last. You remember that odd-spoken old gentleman who was slung up in the top of the tunnel and spoke so sharply to Midwink? When I was on my way back he invited me to go and play chess with him one evening next week. Should I take the invitation seriously or is he a bit cracked? Who is he, anyway?"

Sophie turned to look at him incredulously.

"Don't you know?"

"Of course I don't know." Simon gave her a good-humored pat on the shoulder. "Don't forget I've only just arrived in London. I'm not such an almanac as you, my bright girl. Who is he, then?"

Sophie burst into a fit of laughter which lasted her as far as the servants' entrance to Battersea Castle. "Why," she gasped, wiping the tears of merriment from her eyes, "he's the Duke of Battersea, that's all! Certainly you must keep the appointment—his feelings would be hurt if you didn't."

She gave Simon a quick goodnight hug, and he heard her laughing again as she ran down the tunnel and out of sight.

6

When Simon returned to his lodgings the following evening he saw Miss Dido Twite in her nightgown looking out rather forlornly from the front window into the twilit street. Her face brightened immediately at sight of him and as he entered the house she put her head around her bedroom door.

"Wotcher my cully," she greeted him hoarsely but joyfully.

"Hallo, brat. What's the matter with you?" Simon inquired. She was flushed, and had a long red stocking wound around her throat.

"I have the quinsy," Dido croaked, "and Ma and Pa and Penny-lope and Aunt Poke and Aunt Tinty and *everybody* has gone off to Theobalds' Fair and I'm *that* put about and blue-deviled. Mean, hateful things they are—I wish they was all dead!" She stamped her bare foot on the floor and her lip quivered. "There was to be a Flaming Lady, too, and a Two-Headed Sheep and Performing Fleas and a G-giant C-carnivorous Crocodile."

"Here, don't you think you ought to be in bed?" said Simon, anxious to avert an explosion of tears which seemed imminent. "I'm sure if you have the quinsy you shouldn't be running about in your nightgown. Come on, I'll tuck you up."

"Will you stay and play cribbage with me?" asked Dido instantly.

"All right—only jump in quickly."

She retired through the doorway to a very untidy groundfloor bedchamber evidently shared by the two sisters, for, as well as Dido's meager collection of playthings, it contained curling tongs, copies of the *Ladies' Magazine,* and a great quantity of frilly garments strewn about in a state of disrepair, which plainly belonged to Penelope.

"Now you sit *there,*" ordered Dido, jumping into a skimpy disheveled bed and patting the coverlet. "Here's the cribbage board. Shall we play for money?"

"No, we certainly shall not," said Simon reprovingly. "Besides, I don't for one moment suppose that you have any."

"No, I haven't a tosser to my kick," Dido said, bursting out laughing. "What a hum it would have been if you'd won! Come on—you can start."

They played for an hour, Dido winning all the time, largely because she was prepared to cheat in the most unabashed manner. Then she began to get restless and peevish, and suggested they change over to loo. Simon, who thought she ought to get some rest, proposed that he should straighten her covers and leave her to try and go to sleep, but she raised vehement objections.

"I don't *want* to go to sleep! I don't *want* to be left alone! There's too many people come into this house at night, walking about and bumping on the stairs."

"I don't believe there's a soul except us," said Simon. "You're not scared of ghosts, are you?"

"I ain't afeared of *anything,*" said Dido with spirit. "I jist don't like people walking about on the stairs and bumping. They clanks, too, sometimes."

"Shall I get you something to eat or drink?" Simon suggested.

Dido thought she would like a drink of hot milk. "Ma said she'd leave a mug of milk in the kitchen, but I'd sooner you hotted it. My throat feels like someone's been at it with sandpaper." She gave him a pitiful grin, looking more than ever like a small, molting sparrow.

Simon found the Twites' kitchen, a huge gloomy room in the basement. The mug of milk was on the table, but it took some hunting to discover a clean saucepan. The fire in the range was very low and the coal scuttle empty; he returned to Dido and asked where the coal was kept.

"In the cellar. Door's back o' the pantry. Mind how you go down the steps, they're steep," she croaked. "Ma won't let me go down there."

There were some half-used candles on the kitchen dresser. Simon lit one, took the hod, and went down the steep, narrow cellar stairs. There was another door at the foot, which was locked, but the key was in the lock. He opened this and cautiously entered the darkness beyond, holding his candle high. His foot struck against something metallic which clinked on the stone floor. He lowered the candle and was astonished to see a musket—and another—dozens of them, neatly stacked. And beyond the muskets were barrels of a greyish substance which Simon, by feel and sniff, holding the candle at a safe distance, identified as gunpowder. The room was a regular arsenal!

He found a heap of coal in one corner. Thoughtfully he filled his hod and returned to the kitchen, locking the cellar door behind him again. While he mended the fire and waited for the milk to heat he pondered over this discovery. No wonder Dido heard people bumping and clanking on the stairs! No doubt about it, the Twites must be Hanoverian plotters, bent on removing good King James from the throne, and bringing in the young pretender, Bonnie Prince Georgie from over the water.

The milk came to the boil and, remembering Mrs. Cobb's Special, he shook in some aniseed and took the mug to Dido. She sipped the hot drink gratefully while he beat up her pillows and straightened the blankets with clumsy good will.

"Now you must try to sleep," he ordered when the mug was empty.

"You've got to stay with me till I go off," she countered. She looked hot-cheeked and heavy-eyed, ready to fall asleep at any moment.

"Very well," said Simon. "I'll blow out the candle."

"No, don't do that. Put it over on that cupboard where it won't shine in my eyes."

"Lie down, then." She curled up, sighing, with her back to him, and he placed the candle on the cupboard. As he did so his attention was caught by a small drawing pinned on the wall. He held the light close and saw that it was a sketch portrait of Dido, done roughly but full of life and animation. She was sitting on the front steps, eating a piece of bread and jam. Simon let out an exclamation under his breath and studied the picture intently. The style of drawing was unmistakable: it could be by no other hand than that of Gabriel Field. He looked at the lower right-hand corner where the doctor always signed with his initials, but saw that the whole corner of the paper had been neatly removed by somebody's thumbnail.

He put the candle down and returned to Dido, intending to question her, but she was so drowsy he had not the heart. "Kind," she whispered hoarsely. "Nobody else . . ." Her voice died out. She took a firm hold of Simon's hand and sank into sleep. In any case, what would be the use of questioning her? She would only tell lies about it. Best to mention it to Mr. Twite in the morning—it offered complete proof that Dr. Field had been in the house and seen Dido.

Had Dr. Field stumbled on some evidence of the Hanoverian plot and been put out of the way?

Dido stirred and suddenly opened her eyes.

"Where's your kitty?" she muttered.

"I've lent it to a lady called Mrs. Cobb."

"Why?"

"To catch mice for her."

Dido lay silent. Presently a large tear rolled out from under her closed eyelid.

"What's the matter?"

"First the donkey went—then the kitty went—next *you'll* go. I don't have anyone nice to play with—they allus leaves."

"I shan't leave," Simon soothed her. "You go back to sleep." But as the words left him it suddenly occurred to him to wonder what would happen if the Twites realized that he had seen the arms in the cellar. Would he, like Dr. Field, mysteriously disappear?

Dido's eyelids flickered open, then shut once more. Her breathing slowly became deep and even, her clutch on his hand loosened. Fifteen minutes went by and then he judged it safe to slip his hand free and stand up. As he did so she moved and muttered in her sleep, "Can't tell, you see. Pa would larrup me."

"Never mind," said Simon softly, "I think I know." And he tiptoed from the room.

Simon took a long time to go to sleep. He lay awake worrying, and woke next day with his problem still unsolved. His first impulse had been to inquire his way to the office of the Bow Street constabulary and put the whole matter before them. What would happen then? There would be commotion, uproar, publicity—the Twites would be arrested, no doubt, the guns and ammunition removed, but would he be any nearer discovering what had happened to Dr. Field? He doubted it. After much pondering he decided to keep his own counsel a bit longer, and to watch the Twites even more closely.

To this end, when, as he ate his breakfast, he heard a violent quarrel break out on the stairs, he went quietly onto the landing and stood listening by the banisters out of sight.

"I'll teach you to leave keys in doors!" Mrs. Twite was crying angrily. "Didn't I tell you to see to the fire and lock the cellar before we set out? Oh, you nasty little minx, you! I'll wager you never even fetched the coal. Oh, you hussy, you! All you cared about was prinking and powdering and sticking on beauty spots!"

Simon heard what sounded like a hearty box on the ear followed by an angry shriek from Penelope.

"Leave me be, Ma! Pa, make her leave me be or I declare I'll leave home. I won't stay here to be abused!"

"Best leave her be, then, Ella my dove."

"Hold your tongue, Abednego!"

There followed the sound of a door slamming. Simon waited a moment or two, then ran quietly downstairs.

By the front door he came face to face with Mr. Twite.

"Ah, it's our distinguished young Raphael, our Leonardo-to-be," said Mr. Twite with a wide smile which seemed almost to meet around the back of his head while leaving the upper half of his face quite undisturbed. "I trust you are rejoicing in the pursuit of your studies? Art, art, a hard but rewarding taskmaster!" Evidently rather pleased with the sound of these last words, he repeated them over to himself, shutting his eyes and opening his mouth very wide at each syllable, pronouncing "rewarding" like "guarding." Meanwhile Simon waited for an opportunity to ask about the sketch.

"I delay you," said Mr. Twite, opening his eyes and giving Simon a very sharp look.

"No, sir. I was going to ask how Dido does this morning."

"Poorly, poorly. A delicate sprite," sighed Mr. Twite. "Dido Twite: a delicate sprite," he chanted, to the air of "Three Blind Mice." "It is the curse of our family, young man, to be afflicted by spirits too strong for our bodies."

Simon thought that if Dido were given rather more food, and warmer clothes, and in general more care and attention, her body would be equal to maintaining its spirit, but he did not say so.

"In point of fact," Mr. Twite confided, "the poor child is quite feverish—my wife has just sent along to the pharmacy for a drop of Tintagel water."

"Is that young Thingummy?" called the sharp voice of Mrs. Twite, and she came out of the kitchen, attired for the morning in plum-colored plush. Directing at Simon a smile as glittering as it was insincere, she exclaimed, "It must have been you, dear boy, who heated up a mug of milk for our little one last night."

"Yes it was, ma'am. She didn't fancy it cold, so I heated it and put in a pinch of aniseed. I hope I did nothing wrong?"

"Not a bit, dear boy. *Not* a bit. It was a truly Samaritan act."

"The Samaritans came in two by two,
And paused to bandage the kangaroo—"

sang Mr. Twite.

"*Will* you be quiet, Abednego! I do hope, Mr. Thingummy," pursued Mrs. Twite, looking at Simon very attentively, "that you weren't put to too much *trouble* about it—I hope you didn't have to mend the fire, or fetch coals, or anything of *that* kind?"

"No trouble, ma'am," Simon said. Luckily Mrs. Twite took this to mean that he had not had to fetch coal. "Penny must have told the truth, then," she murmured, glancing significantly at her husband. "She forgot to take the key, but no harm's done."

"She'd better not forget it again, or she'll have a taste of my hoboy."

Simon seized the chance, when Mrs. Twite had retired, of asking who had drawn the little sketch of Dido that hung in her room.

"Sketch of Dido, my boy?" Mr. Twite looked vague. "Is there such a thing? I confess I do not recall it but surrounded as we are by talent, it may be by any of a dozen friends."

"I'll show it to you," Simon said eagerly.

"Later, later, my dear fellow." Mr. Twite held up a restraining hand. "This evening, perhaps. For here comes the lad with the Tintagel water, and Aesculapius must rule supreme." He gently shoved Simon out of the front door as the boy Tod came up the steps with a large black bottle.

That evening Simon was washing out his shirt in a pail of water when Tod opened his door without knocking, and remarked, "Young Dido's calling for you and Aunt Twite says, can you sit with her?"

"Very well." Simon left his shirt soaking. Tod muttered, "Can't think why she wants *you* . . ."

"Oh, there you are, Mr. Thingummy. I declare," exclaimed Mrs. Twite, who looked flushed and irritable, "I'm clean distracted with that child so feverish as she is; keeps trying to get out of bed, and Penelope gone out to goodness knows where, and a meeting of the Glee Society in half an hour. She's been calling for you, dear boy, so if you would just sit with her till she goes off . . ."

"Of course I will," Simon said.

He found Dido in a high fever, throwing herself restlessly about in her bed, muttering random remarks, singing odd snatches of songs. When he took her hand she quieted somewhat and lay back on the pillow.

"Hallo, brat," said Simon. "Do you want to play cards?"

"Too hot," she muttered. "Tell story."

Mrs. Twite put her head around the door long enough to nod gracious approval, and went quickly back to her Glee Society preparations. Simon racked his brains for a story. Then he hit on the notion of telling his adventures during the years when he had lived in his cave in the forest of Willoughby Chase, playing hide-and-seek with the wolves all winter long. This answered famously. Dido left off her restless fidgeting and settled down, holding on to his finger, listening in languid content.

"I'd like to go there . . ." she whispered.

"I expect you will someday."

Her eyes opened in a drowsy flicker. "Will you take me?"

"Yes, very likely, if you are good and go to sleep now."

"Promise?"

"Very well."

Her eyes closed and she slept. Simon carefully withdrew his hand and tiptoed across the room to re-examine the little sketch. But it was gone. Annoyed at not having anticipated this and showed it to Mr. Twite in the morning, he tried to open the door but found it locked. Since he did not like to knock and risk waking Dido he found himself a prisoner; having searched the room for some occupation and rejected the chance of reading numerous copies of the *Maids' Wives' and Widows' Penny Magazine,* he went philosophically to sleep, curled up on the floor.

He woke to find Mr. Twite shaking him.

"*So* sorry, my dear boy, a most unfortunate oversight. My wife thought you had already retired. No doubt you will wish to do so directly."

"Thank you," said Simon, yawning. Then he recollected the sketch. "Mr. Twite, that little drawing of Dido—the one that hung just there—"

"No, no, dear boy, no picture hung there. You imagined it, I daresay—yes, yes, your fancy is full of pictures, it is most natural."

"But I saw—"

"Ah, we artists," said Mr. Twite, waving him out of the door. "Always at the mercy of our visions. By the way," he added in quite another tone, "have you seen my daughter Penelope by any chance?"

"I'm afraid not, sir."

"Strange—most strange. Where can she have got to? Doubtless she will turn up, but it is vexatious. Ah well, I'll keep you no longer from the arms of Morpheus."

Dido was feverish for several days and Simon sat with her each evening until she was pronounced well enough to get up and lie outside on the patch of thistly grass by the river.

"I shan't be able to sit and tell you stories this evening," said Simon, finding her so placed one morning as he went off.

"Why not?"

"Because I shan't be home till late."

"Why? Where are you going? To a circus?" Dido asked with instant suspicion.

"No, no. When I go to a circus I'll take you too. I'm going to play chess with an old gentleman."

"Stupid stuff," said Dido, her interest waning. "*I* wouldn't care to do so. Did you know Penny had run off? She left a note saying she wouldn't be put upon. You should have heard Ma create."

Simon recollected that he had not seen Penelope for several days. He could not feel any sense of loss at her departure.

"P'raps Ma'll make some togs for me, now," Dido said hopefully, echoing Simon's thought. Then she added, "Where're you playing chess, anyways?"

"At Battersea Castle," Simon called over his shoulder as he walked off. "Good-by, brat. See you tomorrow."

"Mr. Cobb," Simon said that evening as he mended the springs of a lady's perch-phaeton. "What would you do if you thought you had discovered a Hanoverian plot?"

Mr. Cobb lowered the wash leather with which he was polishing the panels and regarded Simon with a very shrewd expression.

"Me boy," he said, "it's all Lombard Street to a China orange that I'd turn a blind eye and do nothing about it. Yes, yes, I know—" raising a quelling hand—"I know the Hanoverians are a crew of fire-breathing traitors who want to turn good King James, bless him, off the throne and bring in some flighty German boy. But, I ask you, what do they actually *do*? Nothing. It's all a lot of talk and moonshine, harmless as a kettle on a guinea pig's tail. Why trouble about them when they trouble nobody?"

Simon wondered whether Mr. Cobb would think them so harmless if he were to see the contents of the Twites' cellar. But, just as he was opening his mouth to speak of this the Chelsea Church clock boomed out the hour of nine and he had to hurry off to Battersea Castle.

He took the main way, over Chelsea Bridge and through the great gates beyond it. A tree-bordered avenue led to the castle, which rose like some fabulous pink flower among the encircling gas flares.

"Oo the devil are you and where the devil d'you think you're going?" growled a voice ahead of him. A burly man came out of a porter's lodge halfway along the avenue and halted Simon by pressing a button which caused two crossed lances to rise out of the ground, barring the road.

"The Duke has invited me to play chess with him," Simon said.

"Play chess with a ragged young tyke like you? A likely story," the gatekeeper sneered. As a matter of fact it *was* a likely story, since the Duke made friends with all kinds of odd characters, and this the man knew quite well, but he hoped to wring some gate money out of Simon.

"I'm not ragged and the Duke is expecting me," Simon said calmly. "Let me in, please."

"*Ho,* no! I'm not so green as to let riffraff and flash coves in, to prig whatever they can mill! I'm not lowering that barricade for you, no, not if you was to go down on your benders to me. Not if you was to offer me so much as half a guinea!"

Simon remained silent and the man said angrily, "Not if you was to offer me a *whole* guinea, I wouldn't open it."

"I shan't do that," Simon said.

"Oh? And why not, my young shaver?"

"Because you'll have to open it anyway. The Duchess's carriage is just behind you."

The gatekeeper swung around with an oath. True enough, the carriage, which Simon had observed leaving the castle as he reached the lodge, was pulling up smoothly just behind the man, and the coachman was crying impatiently, "Jump to it, there, Daggett, d'you think her Grace wants to wait all night?"

Red with suppressed emotion, Daggett hastened to obey.

Sophie, who was sitting in the carriage opposite her Grace, holding a reticule, a telescope, and a mah-jongg set, dimpled a smile at Simon, and the Duchess inquired, "Is that your young friend, Sophie? He looks a very personable lad."

"Yes, ma'am," said Sophie.

The Duchess addressed Simon. "So you're the young man who is kindly coming to play chess with William and keep him amused while I go to the opera? It is very obliging of you. William detests opera—and I only find it tolerable if I play mah-jongg with Sophie while the singing is going on. But of course one has one's box and must attend regularly."

"I hope you have a pleasant evening, ma'am," Simon said politely.

"Thank you, my dear boy. We shall meet again, I trust. A delightful face," the Duchess went on, speaking to Sophie as the carriage rolled away. "You have excellent taste, Sophie dear."

"Thank you, your Grace."

The main entrance to the castle lay up a tremendous flight of curving steps. At the top stood two haughty bewigged footmen in cream-and-gold livery with rose-colored buttons.

"Good evening," Simon said civilly. "I've come to play chess with the Duke."

Evidently they had been told to expect him. One of them led him in through a lofty hall, up another flight of stairs, and across a great black-and-white-tiled anteroom to a pair of doors which he threw open, announcing, "The young person, your Grace."

The room Simon entered was a large library with fireplaces on either side. The Duke jumped from a chair by one fireside and came hurrying forward. He was elegantly dressed tonight in satin knee breeches and a velvet jacket, but still looked absent-minded and untidy—the old-fashioned wig he wore was twisted askew, so was his cravat, and one of his velvet cuffs was covered in ash.

"Ah, this is a pleasure!" he exclaimed. "I have been greatly looking forward to our game." He bustled about, pulling forward a comfortable chair and ringing several bells.

"You'll take a little something?" he inquired. "Blackcurrant brandy? Prune wine? Scrimshaw, bring the chess set. Jabwing, prune wine and biscuits."

The Duke's chess set was very beautiful. The pieces were of greenish glass, cunningly twisted and carved. The Duke set them out lovingly on a leather board, polishing each one on his cravat. The white men were clear right through, the black were veined with streaks of darker glass.

They began to play, and it did not take Simon long to discover that his Grace was not a very good player. He tended to start well with some bold moves, but then his attention would wander; he would jump up hastily to search for a quotation in a book, or to examine a patch of lichen on one of the burning logs in the hearth.

"You play very well, my boy," the Duke said, after Simon had won two out of three games. "Who taught you?"

"A friend of mine, sir," Simon said, sighing. "A Dr. Gabriel Field."

The Duke's face lit up. "Ah, Dr. Field! He is an excellent player, is he not? And a dear fellow. Where is the good doctor? I have not seen him this age."

"You know Dr. Field?" Simon gazed at him in astonishment.

"Why, yes. I met him at the Academy of Art."

"Rivière's? Where I learn painting?"

"Oh, you learn painting, do you, my boy? I am not surprised to hear it, for you have the face of an artist. Yes, I met Dr. Field at Rivière's—I am one of the patrons, you know, Marius Rivière was married to my aunt. I often drop in at the academy. The good doctor and I have many interests in common; he has advised me on several pieces of scientific research, and helped clean my pictures."

"Clean pictures, your Grace?" Simon was momentarily puzzled.

"Family pictures, old masters, that have become darkened with age." Simon nodded; Dr. Field had given him some instruction in the processes of picture-cleaning on his last visit.

"Indeed," the Duke went on, "I wish he would return, for he was halfway through cleaning Rivière's famous painting of a wolf hunt and I long to have it completed. See, I will show you."

He led the way to the far end of the library—a good hundred yards off. Here he turned, blowing a shrill blast on a small gold whistle. One of the footmen came running from the door.

"Jabwing, light some more tapers, please, and then bring my gruel."

Soon half a hundred candles had been kindled and by their clear blaze Simon was able to study a large canvas occupying most of the end wall of the room. The picture represented a hunt in a snowy wood, and he could see that it was by the hand of a master. A group of hunters, richly dressed in costumes of thirty years ago, were galloping to the help of two men and some hounds who were being attacked by a pack of wolves.

Half the picture had been cleaned and restored, the other half was still dark with grease and grime, so that hunters and wolves alike seemed to be plunging into a black chasm.

"It certainly needs cleaning," Simon remarked. "It looks very old."

"In fact the picture is only thirty years old," the Duke told him. "But it was a great favorite of my father, the fourth Duke, and he would always have it hanging by the fireplace where he used to sit in the evenings. With the smoke from the fire, and the great pipe he smoked, the picture became villainously begrimed. The fair-haired lady on the white horse is Lady Helen Bayswater, my aunt, who was married to the painter; he himself is one of the men on foot and it is thought that his daughter, too, is somewhere in the picture, the part still uncleaned. She was my cousin; they say she was very beautiful but I never met her. She met my younger brother by chance when both were taking the waters at Epsom, they fell in love, and made a runaway match of it. And they both died in the Hanoverian wars." He sighed deeply. "Young Justin, their son, is the last of the line, as you can see from the family tree over there."

Simon looked where he was bidden and saw a chart which meant little to him. Trying to turn the Duke's thoughts in a more cheerful direction—for he looked very melancholy—Simon suggested, "I could perhaps go on cleaning the picture for you, your Grace, if you like. Dr. Field taught me how."

"Would you, my boy? I should like it of all things! When could you begin?"

"Tomorrow, sir, if you like."

"Famous!" declared his Grace. "I will tell my steward to have the glass removed again—we had it off for Field and then put it back when he stopped coming—and to procure you all the cleaning materials that you may need. Upon my word, I can't wait to see those poor dirty wolves smartened up and made neat."

He began pointing out objects in the murk at the foot of the canvas, and Simon leaned forward, intently studying the untouched area. While he was doing so his eye caught a movement reflected in the picture glass from the opposite end of the room.

Jabwing the footman had brought in a small tray with a basin of gruel which he placed on the chess table. He then stopped and removed something from the Duke's chair; quietly, and looking about to make sure he was unobserved (but he did not see Simon watching him in the glass) he bore this object across the room and slipped it into the pocket of Simon's old frieze jacket which had been left lying on a chair. Then he withdrew silently until, when he was just beside the door, he cleared his throat and said in a loud voice, "Your Grace's gruel is ready."

"Thank you, Jabwing, thank you," the Duke said absently. "You may go—unless—do you take gruel, my boy? No? You are certain? My cook has a capital way of making it with white wine and sugar—no? That will be all, then, Jabwing."

The Duke returned to the fireside and swallowed his gruel, happily discussing the cleansing operation.

Simon meanwhile quietly investigated his jacket pocket to discover what the footman had put in it. His fingers encountered a large, round, hard object which, on being withdrawn, proved to be the Duke's gold hunter watch, set with turquoises, which had been left on the arm of his chair.

Simon stared at this article for a moment, with his brow knitted, and then placed it on a small side-table among a number of crystal ornaments. He was curious to see what would happen.

"I only wish Dr. Field would return, he would be so delighted to find that you were helping me," the Duke was

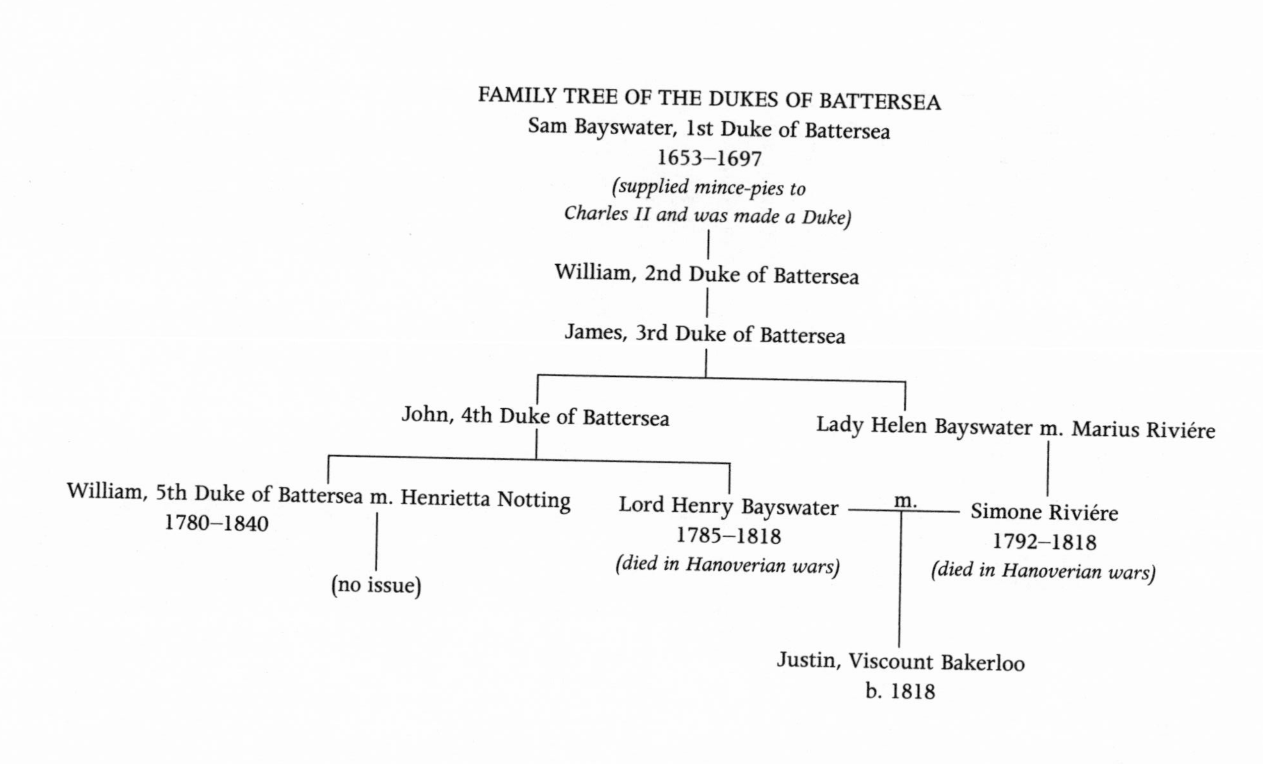
FAMILY TREE OF THE DUKES OF BATTERSEA
Sam Bayswater, 1st Duke of Battersea
1653–1697
(supplied mince-pies to
Charles II and was made a Duke)
William, 2nd Duke of Battersea
James, 3rd Duke of Battersea
John, 4th Duke of Battersea
Lady Helen Bayswater m. Marius Riviére
William, 5th Duke of Battersea m. Henrietta Notting
1780–1840
(no issue)
Lord Henry Bayswater
1785–1818
(died in Hanoverian wars)
m.
Simone Riviére
1792–1818
(died in Hanoverian wars)
Justin, Viscount Bakerloo
b. 1818

saying. "He is forever telling me that my pictures need attention, and his own time is limited, poor fellow."

"Speaking of time," Simon said politely, "I think I should be going, your Grace. It must be late."

"Should you, my boy? What o'clock is it, then? I'll ring for someone to show you out."

By the time Jabwing reappeared the Duke had discovered the loss of his watch and was hunting for it fretfully.

"Jabwing, Jabwing, I've lost my watch, what time is it?"

"Eleven past, your Grace."

"Is it, indeed? I'd no notion it was so late. Jabwing, show the young gentleman out, then come back and find my watch for me."

Jabwing brought Simon's jacket and, as he did so, contrived to turn it upside down, as if by accident, and give it a smart shake. A round object shot out of the pocket and fell with a loud rap to the marble floor.

"Why!" exclaimed Jabwing in pretended astonishment, "isn't that your Grace's watch?"

But he spoke a moment too soon, before he had seen what it was.

"No it isn't, Jabwing," snapped the Duke testily. "Where are your eyes? Any dolt can see that it is a hard-boiled egg!"

"My breakfast," explained Simon, quietly recovering and pocketing the egg.

"And I should like to know," the Duke went on indignantly, still addressing Jabwing, "what you mean by the outrageous suggestion that my watch would be in the pocket of a visitor, eh? Explain yourself, my man!"

Jabwing was covered with confusion.

"Entirely a mistake, your Grace—very sorry, very sorry indeed. Only on account of the gentleman's being a—a rather a *shabby* young gentleman—and the egg's being so —so round, you know—wouldn't for the world give any offense—"

"Well, you have given it, blockhead, and it makes it no better to cast aspersions on the young gentleman's clothes. I've a good mind to dismiss you. Don't let such a thing occur again or you'll be sent back to Chippings! Good night, then, my dear boy, I shall look forward with impatience to our next meeting. Why, there *is* my watch after all," he continued, catching sight of it on the table, "I must have laid it there while showing you the Rivière. And, dear me, how late it is!"

Jabwing ushered Simon out and down the great stairway without a word, but his face spoke volumes and if looks could have done it there would have been a banana skin waiting to trip Simon on every step. As he threw open the hall doors he hissed one word, "Interloper!" into Simon's ear, and then slammed the door behind him with an insulting crash.

Simon walked down the long drive in a very thoughtful frame of mind. He half wished that he had not suggested coming to clean the picture, but he had taken a liking to the Duke, who seemed a kind old fellow and rather lonely. It was plain, though, that it would be necessary to keep a lookout against such hostile acts as that of Jabwing, who had clearly hoped to get Simon turned out and discredited as a common thief. It was almost, Simon thought, remembering the malevolent gatekeeper and the sour looks of Midwink the valet, as if someone had an interest in keeping him out of Battersea Castle. But why should that be?

Puzzling over this new problem he went home to bed.

7

One morning, several weeks later, Dido waylaid Simon. She had recovered from her fever, but still looked pale, and was shaken from time to time by a dry cough.

"You never plays with me nowadays," she complained. There was a forlorn droop to her mouth, and Simon took pity on her.

"I'll tell you what, brat, I shall be free on Sunday afternoon, for Mr. Cobb's yard is closed then and I'll have finished the other job I'm working on"—he meant the cleaning of the Rivière, which was nearing completion—"so I'll take you on an outing. What shall it be? A trip down the river on a pleasure boat? Or shall we go into the country—take our dinners and hunt for highwaymen in Blackheath Woods?"

Dido was enchanted at this offer. Her eyes sparkled and she began to jump up and down on the dirty front steps, hanging on to Simon's arm in a very exhausting manner, until a fit of coughing obliged her to desist.

"Clapham Fair! Can we go to Clapham Fair? Pa said he

wouldn't take me, he allus has forty winks on Sunday afternoons, and Ma goes to the Lady Triangulists' Social, and Penny-lope's gone off . . . They say there's a talking pig that'll answer any question you ask! And there's whirligigs and flying boats and giddy-go-rounds and Lambeth cakes and treacle sticks!"

"All right, all right, don't deafen me, brat! You shall go to the fair. Only for my sake, will you put on a clean pinafore when we go, and wash your face?"

"Oh, stuff!" Dido put out her tongue at him between the railings. Simon waved a hand to her and went whistling away down the street.

The Duke of Battersea was not at home that evening, having been inveigled, for once, into attending a performance at the opera with his lady. Sophie, who sometimes slipped into the library for a chat when Simon was there, had left a note tucked among his cleaning tools, informing him that she also would be out, escorting her mistress. (For fear of being bored, the Duchess would go nowhere without a supply of amusements, reading matter, and embroidery things, which it was Sophie's duty to carry.) The party would not be home until a late hour.

Simon was disappointed not to see Sophie, but the absence of his Grace's somewhat fidgety companionship made it easier to get on with the job, and he applied himself with a will, whistling gently between his teeth as he uncovered more and more of the large picture until there was only a patch as big as a top-hat left to clean.

"Hilloo," remarked a supercilious voice behind his

shoulder after an hour or two had gone by. "How's the paint-scrubber getting on?" He turned to see young Lord Bakerloo surveying the cleaning operations somewhat scornfully. He seemed disposed to linger, however, rocking to and fro on his heels, picking up first one, then another of the cleaning tools until Simon longed to tell him to leave them be.

"How's old Fur-nose?" he presently inquired.

Simon replied that Dr. Furneaux seemed in the best of health, and civilly asked after Lord Bakerloo's arm.

"Can you keep a secret?" said Justin.

"Of course."

"Well, so can I. Mum's the word." Justin doubled up with laughter at his own wit and added, "You won't see me at that old academy again for a long, long time, I can tell you."

Simon made no reply to this, but quietly got on with his work, while Justin wandered about behind him, occasionally singing snatches of a ballad which seemed to consist principally of the refrain:

"Hip-hap, habble-dabble-oh,
Shall we go
To Haberdashers' Row?"

until Simon felt there was no place in London that he less wished to visit.

"Devilish dull here, this evening, ain't it?" Justin presently broke off to say. He yawned until his face seemed ready to split. "I almost wish I'd gone to the opera with the old gudgeons—not that Aunt Hettie asked me," he added sourly. "I believe Buckle peached on me; said I hadn't finished my lessons. By the bye, Uncle Bill charged me with a message to you. I was to ask if you was free to play chess with him on Sunday. Getting jumped-up in the world, aren't we? My oh me, playing chess with the gentry and nobil-itee."

"Do you mean his Grace the Duke invited me?" Simon asked, ignoring the sneer in the last sentence.

"O' course I do. Uncle Bill Battersea, mad as a hatter, see, growing much fatter, see, oh, devilish good. I'm a wit, I am!"

Simon disagreed, but kept his opinion to himself. He said, "Will you please tell his Grace that I thank him kindly for the invitation but that I shan't be able to accept."

"Blest if I see why *I* should carry your messages," Justin said. "Why can't you write him a note? Or can't you write?" he added rudely.

Simon checked an irritable retort, calmly wrote a note on a page of his sketchbook, folded it into a cocked hat, and laid it on his Grace's fireside table.

"Fancy that! We *can* write!" said Justin with heavy sarcasm. Plainly he was spoiling for a quarrel, and longed to provoke Simon into setting about him. Simon, instead, began to feel rather sorry for him; he seemed lonely and bored, disappointed at not being taken to the opera, and very much at a loose end.

"Anyway, why *can't* you come on Sunday?" Justin

inquired with the persistence of a buzz fly. "It ain't very polite to turn down Uncle Bill's invitation."

"I'm taking Dido Twite to Clapham Fair."

"*That* little bag of bones? What the dickens do you want to do that for?" Justin exclaimed, truly astonished. "She's as dirty as a gutter perch, and got no more manners or gratitude than a hedge fish."

Simon remarked mildly that he had promised Dido a treat long since, and she had chosen to go to the Fair.

"Well, I wish I was coming instead of Dido," Justin remarked frankly. "It's a prime good fair, I can tell you. I sneaked out last year and went with Jem the stableboy, but now old Buckle-and-Thong's living in the castle, keeping such a tight eye on me, I daresay I shan't be allowed."

"You're welcome to come with me if you can get permission," Simon said.

Justin's face lit up. "*Could* I? Oh, that'd be spanking. But," he added gloomily, "it's no use asking, for if Buckle heard I was going with you and Dido Twite he'd never allow it. It'd be the monkey's allowance, sure as you're alive. He don't permit me to associate with *low-born* persons. He's a sight stricter than Uncle Bill! I'd slip off anyways, but they keep me so devilish short of blunt that I've hardly two groats to rub together. I suppose you couldn't lend me a cartwheel, could you?"

"Yes, all right," Simon said calmly. "But I shall tell your uncle that I am taking you, you know. I daresay he'll have no objection, but I don't want to do anything behind his Grace's back." He handed over the coin.

"If you *tell* him, we're making the whole arrangement for Habbakuk," Justin said discontentedly. "Surly old Buckle will find some way to stop my going, I'll bet you a borde. How I hate him, the cheese-faced old screw!"

"Lord Bakerloo!" said an acidly angry voice just behind his back. He whirled round. Mr. Buckle stood there.

"What are you doing in the library, pray?" Buckle said. "You know that his Grace left strict instructions you were not to consort with the cleaning boy and hinder him from his work. Back to your studies, my lord, if you please."

"Oh, very well," replied Justin sulkily, and began to slouch away, making a grimace at Simon. Mr. Buckle, who had hitherto ignored Simon, now cast one sharply penetrating and strangely malignant glance at him. His eye moved on from Simon to the picture, completely clean at last. Something about it suddenly seemed to attract his very particular attention; he stared at it fixedly for a moment or two, then glanced at Simon again, with eyes dilated, then back at the picture. "Good God!" he exclaimed under his breath, gave Simon a last hard scrutiny, and hurried after his charge.

Simon, very much surprised, inspected the picture attentively himself to try and discover what had fixed the tutor's interest. The last section to be cleaned was the portrait of a dark-haired boy on a pony. There seemed nothing odd about him that Simon could see; in the end he gave up the puzzle and began putting his tools together, preparatory to departure. At this moment he heard a confusion of voices outside the door and a group of persons burst into the room, all talking at once.

The Duke was in front, with her Grace the Duchess, followed by Midwink, the sour-faced valet, and Sophie, besides a couple of footmen and an elderly lady's maid, who was alternately wringing her hands, examining a hole in a large opera cloak she carried, and lamenting at the top of her voice: "Oh, my lady, my lady! Cloth of copper tissue embroidered with fire-opals! Fourteen guineas the inch! Ruined! And lucky you was not to be all burnt in your seats! Oh, why wasn't I there?"

"Nonsense, Fibbins, we did quite well without you," the Duchess replied briskly. "Now, Scrimshaw, don't stand about gaping, but bring refreshment! We have all had an unpleasant experience and our spirits need sustaining. His Grace wants prune brandy and Stilton, while I will take a glass of black-currant wine and a slice of angel cake. So will Sophie, I'm sure, won't you, my dear? Indeed, without your cool head I don't know where we should all have been. We should certainly not be here now."

"No indeed!" interjected his Grace. "Gal's got a head on her shoulders worth two of any of those dunderheaded ushers at Drury Lane. Very much obliged to ye, my dear; shan't forget it in a hurry."

"Oh, truly, my lady, and thank you, your Grace; it was nothing."

Hearing this praise of Sophie, Simon could not resist lingering.

"Hallo, you there, my boy?" his Grace cried, discovering him. "You work while we play, eh? And better it would have been if we'd all stayed at home minding our own business. Here's such an adventure we've been through; only just escaped with our lives, thanks to clever little Miss Sophie here."

"What happened?" Simon asked, no longer attempting to conceal his lively interest.

"Why, my lady wife drags us all off to the opera (and miserable plaguey slow it was, too, I don't mind telling you; I can never make head nor tail of these fellers warbling away about their troubles—pack o' nonsense, if you ask me, when anyone can see they've never wanted for a good dinner in their lives); all of a sudden in the first act we all smell smoke, and next thing you know, the whole of our blessed box is afire, curtains, carpets, and all! And can we get out? No, we can not! Why, do you ask?" (The Duke, in his excitement, had quite thrown off his usual vague air.) "Why, because the box door is locked, and though we shout and call, nobody can find the key! So we should all three have been nicely frizzled for anything anyone could do, if it hadn't been for little miss, here."

"What *did* Sophie do?" Simon asked, absently accepting a slice of cake and a glass of black-currant wine from Scrimshaw.

"Why, she outs with Madam's embroidery, which, as you may know, is a piece of tapestry big enough to cover the end wall of this room, rolls it into a rope, hangs it over the front of the box, and tells me to slide down it!"

"And did you, your Grace?"

"To be sure I did! Haven't had such a famous time since

I was a little feller in nankeen snufflers sliding down the stair rail at Chippings Castle!"

"And did her Grace slide down the rope too?" Simon inquired, much astonished.

"Bless you, no! Took a fit of the vapors at the very idea! So we was all in a flimflam, if Sophie hadn't thrown the tapestry down and called out, 'Hold it tightly by the corners!' So I and half a dozen other gentlemen held it out tight, while her Grace and Sophie jumped into it (one at a time, of course; as it was her Grace's weight nearly pulled my arms out o' the sockets, didn't it, my dear?)."

"Such an indecorous thing to be obliged to do!" sighed her Grace, fanning herself with a piece of cake.

"Yes, and it's my belief that you'd hardly have done it then if little Miss Sophie hadn't given you a smart push from behind, eh, miss? I saw you," said the Duke, grinning at Sophie, who blushed, but defended herself.

"Her Grace was—was hesitating a little, and really there was no time to be lost. The flames were already catching her cloak."

"Ruined! Ten thousand guineas' worth of copper brocade," wailed the lady's maid.

"Oh, be quiet, Fibbins! You should be grateful her Grace herself isn't burnt to a crisp, instead of that miserable cloak I've never liked above half. Yes, and two minutes after they'd jumped, the whole box crashed down into the stalls. What do you think of that, eh?"

Simon then recollected his manners and took his leave, sure that the ducal family would not wish the presence of a stranger after such an alarming adventure.

The Duke clapped him kindly on the back. "Off, are you? How's the picture getting on? What, done already? Come, that's famous; I'd no notion you'd do it so quickly. See, Hettie, doesn't it look better?"

"Indeed, it is a great, great improvement," her Grace said warmly. "I'd no idea that dingy old painting could be made so bright and handsome. Why, good gracious! William, look at this, only look!"

"What, my love? What has surprised you?"

"Look at this girl on the pony!"

"That *girl,* my dove, is a boy; observe his breeches!"

"Girl or boy, what does it matter?" said the Duchess impatiently. "But whichever it is, he or she is the very spit image of Sophie!"

8

It was late that night before Simon returned to his lodgings; the Twites' part of the house was all in darkness and he had to feel his way up the steep stairs by the light of the moon which shone in at the landing window. He did not trouble to light a candle in his room but was about to undress and jump into bed when an unexpected sound made him pause.

The sound, which came from the bed, was a muffled and broken gulping, somewhat resembling the grunts of a small pig.

"Who's there?" Simon said cautiously.

The only reply was a dejected sniff. Beginning to guess what he should see, Simon found and lit his stump of candle; it displayed a small miserable figure curled up on his bed with its face hidden in the pillow.

"Dido! What are you doing up here? What's the matter?"

She raised a tear-stained face and said woefully, "Ma won't let me go to the Fair!"

"Why not? Have you been naughty?"

"No, I never. But she was in a fair tweak about summat Pa said—they was at it hammer and tongs, I heard him shouting that she was under the thumb of her havey-cavey kin and would have us all in the Pongo—and then when I asked about the Fair she just glammered at me and said no."

"Well, you were a dunderhead to ask her when she was cross, weren't you," Simon said, but not unkindly. He sat down on the bed, put his arm around her, and gave her a consoling pat on the back. "Why don't you be extra good for a day or two and then ask her again; it's odds but she'll have forgotten she forbade you."

"N-no," said Dido forlornly. "Acos when I said *why* couldn't I go, she said acos I'd got no warm dresses that were fit to wear outdoors."

"Lord bless us! Can't she buy you something, or make you something? You don't have to keep indoors all winter, surely?"

"She said she couldn't get anything till Friday fortnight when Pa gives her the housekeeping. It's not *fair!*" said Dido passionately. "She was allus favoring Penny—only just afore Penny run off she had a candy-floss shawl and three pair of Manila gloves and a blue-and-white-striped ticking overmantel! Ma jist don't like me, she never buys me *anything!*"

This was true; Simon saw no point in disputing it.

"And that's another reason why Pa was cagging at her," Dido went on. "Acos she'd spent all the housekeeping on Penny's duds and a load of Pictclobbers."

"What are Pictclobbers?" Simon asked, pricking up his ears.

"*I* dunno." Dido was not interested. "They put 'em in the cellar. And now there won't be nothing to eat but lentil bread and fish porridge till Friday fortnit and I can't go to the Fair."

"Would your ma let you go if you had something to wear?"

"She said yes. But she knew I hadn't got nothing, so it was a lot of Habbakuk."

"Oh," said Simon. He reflected. "Well, look, don't be too miserable—I've a friend who might be able to help, she's very clever at making dresses, and perhaps she'd have something of hers that she could alter. I'll ask her tomorrow. So cheer up."

Dido's skinny arms came around his neck in a throttling hug. "*Would* she? Simon, you're a proper nob. I'm sorry I ever put jam on your hair. I think you're a bang-up—*slumdinger!*"

"All right, well, don't get your hopes up too high," he said hastily. "Your ma may not agree, even if I can get something."

"Oh, it's dibs to dumplings she will, if she gets summat for nix," said Dido shrewdly.

"Now you'd better nip back to bed before you get a dusting for being out of your room."

"It's all rug. They're out; Pa's playing his hoboy at Drury Lane and he got tickets for Ma and Aunt Tinty to go tonight."

"Still I expect they'll be in soon; anyway *I* want my sleep."

"Oh, all right, toll-loll," said Dido, whose spirits had risen amazingly. "But I'm nibblish hungry. I'm *fed up* with fish porridge—hateful stuff."

"There's a bit of cheese on the table."

"I've et it."

"Oh, you have, have you? Well, here, take this sausage, and be off, brat, and don't take things that don't belong to you another time."

"Slumguzzle," said Dido impertinently, but she gave him another hug (thereby anointing his hair with sausage) and condescended to leave him in peace.

Just before he went to sleep a drowsy thought flickered through his mind. Dido had said that Mr. Twite was playing his hoboy at Drury Lane. *Drury Lane.* Was not that where the Duke and Duchess and Sophie had met with their misadventure? Was there any connection between the two events?

Next morning, as he ran down the front steps, he saw a small pale face at the downstairs window directing at him a look full of silent appeal. He waved reassuringly but did not stop to speak, as he was late, and, moreover, saw Mrs. Twite approaching with a basket of herrings, presumably for the fish porridge. She gave him a chilly nod, scowled reprovingly at Dido, and passed within. Simon wondered what she would say if she knew Dido had told him that the housekeeping money had been spent on Pictclobbers. What were Pictclobbers, anyway? He was pretty sure they were not coal. Pistols or muskets seemed more likely.

It was a cold, gray November morning, but presently

the sun rose, dispersing the river mists and gilding the last leaves on the trees. Dr. Furneaux ordered his students outside to "paint hay while ze sun shines," as he put it.

Simon was sitting on the riverbank not far from the academy, hard at work on a water-color sketch of Chelsea Bridge with the dreamlike pink towers of Battersea Castle behind it, when a handsome pleasure barge swept under the bridge, traveling upstream with the tide. It passed close to Simon so that he was able to see the Battersea Arms (two squirrels respecting each other, vert, and az., eating mince pies or) embroidered on the sail.

"Good morning, Simon!" a voice called, and he noticed Sophie leaning over the forward rail. She wore a white dress with red ribbons and carried the usual assortment of needments for the Duchess—a basket of shrimps to feed the gulls, a book, a parasol, a battledore and shuttlecock, and a large bundle of embroidery.

Simon waved back and called, "What time shall you be home? Can I see you this evening?"

"We shan't be late," Sophie answered. "His Grace and my lady are off to Hampton Court to take luncheon with his Majesty, but we shall return directly afterwards because my lady is still tired from last night's adventure. I'll come round to Mr. Cobb's at nine—will you be there?"

"That will do famously," Simon called. The Duke, who, dressed in full court regalia, was steering in the stern, saw him and waved so enthusiastically that he nearly dropped his pocket handkerchief overboard.

The day passed pleasantly in the warm autumn sunshine. At noon the students lit a fire and brewed acorn coffee; later, Dr. Furneaux came out and criticized their work. He discussed Simon's picture with ferocity, going into every point, often seizing the brush to alter some detail, until his whiskers were covered with paint.

Gus winked at Simon behind the principal's back and whispered, "Bear up, cully! The more old Fur-nose thinks of you, the more he's into you." Then his eyes widened, looking past Simon, and he exclaimed, "Stap and roast me! What the deuce is the matter with that boat?"

Simon turned to look at the river. A boat was coming from the direction of Hampton Court, but, for a moment, he did not recognize the ducal barge, so strange an appearance did it present. It was creeping along low in the water with hardly any of the hull visible, and the whole craft was curiously wrapped about in folds of material, so that it looked more like a floating parcel than a boat. Somebody had just jumped off it, and as they watched there were three more splashes, and they saw the heads of swimmers making for the shore.

"It's sinking!" exclaimed Gus.

"And the rowers have jumped clear," said Simon, recognizing the cream-and-gold livery of the swimmers. "But where's the Duke and Duchess and Sophie?"

In a moment he saw them as the barge, carried along by the outgoing tide, slowly wallowed past. They were all in the stern, the Duke and Sophie trying to persuade the Duchess to jump for it.

"Indeed you must, ma'am!" implored Sophie. "When

the ship sinks—and she will at any minute!—we shall all be sucked under."

"But I can't swim!" lamented the Duchess. "I shall certainly be drowned, and in my best court dress too—murrey velvet with gold sequins—it will be ruined and it cost over twenty thousand—"

"Hettie, you *must* jump! Never mind the perditioned dress!"

"But it weighs twenty-three pounds—it will sink me like a stone. Oh, help, help, will nobody help us?"

"All right, your Grace!" shouted Simon, pulling off his shirt. "We're coming!"

Half the students of the academy dived joyfully off the bank and swam to the rescue, delighted at such a diversion, and this was just as well, for next minute the barge filled up completely, turned on its side, and precipitated the three passengers into the water. The Duchess would undoubtedly have sunk had not, by great good fortune, her voluminous skirts and petticoats filled with air for a few moments so that she floated on the surface like a bubble while Sophie supported her.

"Dammit!" gasped the Duke. "I can't swim either, come to think! I never—aaaargh!" He disappeared in a welter of bubbles, but luckily Gus and Fothers, forging through the water like porpoises, both reached the spot at that instant and were able to dive and grab him. Meanwhile Simon, Sophie, and half a dozen other students managed to land the Duchess while others swam after the barge and steered it to a sandspit on the far side of Chelsea Bridge.

Dr. Furneaux, meanwhile, after wringing his hands and whiskers alternately, when he saw that the rescue was safely under way, had very sensibly organized some more students into building up a fine blaze from the embers of the noon fire so that the victims of the wreck could warm themselves immediately. The setting sun and the huge bonfire threw a red light over the strange scene, steam rose in clouds from those who had been immersed, while others ran to and fro fetching more branches.

"By Jove!" said the Duke as he stood steaming and emptying water out of his diamond-buckled shoes. "What a scrape, eh? I fancied my number was up that time—so it would have been too, if it weren't for your plucky lads, Furneaux! Much obliged to 'ee all!"

"Indeed, yes!" The Duchess smiled around warmly upon the dripping assembled students. She looked much less bedraggled than anybody, as the upper part of her body had never been submerged, thanks to the speed with which she had been towed to land. "You are a set of brave, good souls. You must all come to dinner at the castle as soon as possible."

Dr. Furneaux beamed with pride and affection for his students. "Yes, yes," he said, "Zey are a set of brave *garçons* when it comes to a tight pinch—it is only ze hard work zey do not always enjoy!"

"What happened to the barge?" Simon asked Sophie as they stood drying themselves. "How did it come to sink?"

"Nobody knows exactly," she answered. "It was certainly all right when we reached Hampton Court. But on the way home it seemed to move heavily in the water and when we had gone a certain way—I do not know where we were—"

"Mortlake, or thereabouts," the Duke put in.

"It seemed to be sinking lower and lower, and suddenly her Grace gave a scream—we were all on deck, but she looked down the companionway and saw there was nearly a foot of water in the cabin, and more coming in. There was a hole in the side! So I had the notion of passing her Grace's tapestry under the hull, over the hole, and pulling it up tight against both sides, to stop the leak. We did so, and it worked tolerably well for quite a long way—"

"Ay, my child, it was a brainwave," the Duke said. "Had it not been for your clever wits 'tis a herring to a ha'penny we'd ha' been shipwrecked at Putney or some such godforsaken spot where we would undoubtedly have perished with not a soul to hear our cries. For you could not have rescued both of us, Sophie my dear, and as for those cowardly jobberknolls of rowers, they were no more use than a fishskin fowling piece—I'll turn every last one of them out of my service, so I will. Where are they?"

The rowers, however, when they reached land, had prudently made off and did not even wait for their dismissal; they were seen at Battersea Castle no more.

"Alas for my tapestry, though," the Duchess sighed. "I fear it will be quite ruined."

"Nonsense, my dear," her husband exclaimed. "We'll have it dried and cleaned, and you'll see it will be as good as new. And even if it ain't *quite* the same, I'd as lief keep it—do you realize that tapestry has saved our lives twice? And each time thanks to adroit little Miss Sophie here? We are much in your debt, my dear."

"Where did you learn to swim so well?" the Duchess inquired.

"Oh, it was nothing, your Graces," Sophie said shyly. "I learnt to swim at the Poor Farm; indeed we were obliged to, with the canal so close by—someone was forever falling in. But please think no more about it my lady. Look, here comes the carriage and I am persuaded your Graces should be taken home *immediately* and be put to bed with three hot bricks each to avoid all danger of an inflammation."

"Quite right, my child, quite right! Hettie! let us be off. Dr. Furneaux, will you bring all your students along to take pot luck with us tomorrow night? Ay, and I've something famous to show you all, my big Rivière canvas which this good boy has cleaned."

Dr. Furneaux gladly accepted on behalf of his students and expressed his eagerness to see the restored painting. Amid hurrahs and waving caps the carriage drove away toward Battersea Castle. As night was now falling fast, the students decided to abandon work and make a party of it. More acorn coffee was brewed; those who had money went and bought potatoes in Chelsea Market to roast in the embers, while those who had none fetched chestnuts from Battersea Park or merely danced minuets and quadrilles by the light of the moon.

When the chimes of the Chelsea Church clock boomed out the hour of nine, Simon recollected his appointment to meet Sophie. He set off at a run, though wondering if the task of caring for her rescued mistress might have prevented Sophie coming out again.

She had not failed him, however. He found her sitting with the Cobb family, helping Mrs. Cobb hem pinafores for Libby while she regaled them all with a lively account of the shipwreck.

Simon asked how the Duke and Duchess did.

"Famously snug," said Sophie. "They both went to bed with hot bricks, and I gave them a dose of the poppy syrup that I made according to Mrs. Cobb's receipt."

"Ay, you can't beat my poppy syrup," said Mrs. Cobb complacently.

"And they were both very kind to me," Sophie went on. "The Duke gave me five guineas and this gold enameled watch—see, Libby, how pretty it is with the blue flowers—and her Grace gave me a week's holiday, besides two beautiful dresses and five lengths of stuff to make things for myself. But what was it you wanted to ask me, Simon?"

Simon explained the troubles of poor Dido Twite, with an unfeeling mother, a diet of fish porridge, and no dress to wear to the Clapham Fair. Sophie's kind eyes misted in sympathy as she listened, and Mrs. Cobb cried, "Well, I declare! Fancy treating a child so! She could have some of Libby's clothes, but they'd be too small, I daresay."

"It's the simplest thing in the world," Sophie said, "I can use some of the stuff her Grace gave me to make the child a dress—it will take no time at all to whip it together if you can give me some idea of her size, Simon."

"Oh no, that's a great deal too good of you," he objected. "I wondered if you'd have some old dress put by that you could cut up for her, Soph."

Sophie however declared that the Duchess had given her so many things she could easily spare some material—"The poor little thing, let her have something really pretty and new for once. There is a blue merino that might be just the thing. Is she dark or fair?"

"She is always so grubby that it is hard to tell," Simon said doubtfully. However he thought the blue merino would do very well.

"I'll make it tomorrow," Sophie promised. "As I've the day off, it's odds but I'll have it finished by the evening."

"Come and do it here," offered Mrs. Cobb. "You'll be company for me, my dear; Cobby's off to Hackney to look at some carriages."

"Soph, you are a Trojan," Simon said. "I made sure you'd be able to help." A bright idea struck him. "If you have the week off you could come to the Fair too, couldn't you? We could make a regular junket of it. It's on Sunday—the day after tomorrow."

"Why, I should love to!" Sophie said, her eyes sparkling at the thought.

They agreed to fix a meeting time and place next evening, when Simon came to fetch the dress.

Dido's problem was now solved but, as Simon walked home after having escorted Sophie to the gates of Battersea Tunnel, he reflected that the cloud of mystery in which he moved seemed to be thickening daily. He wondered if he ought to warn the Duke that danger threatened—if it did—or would that merely raise unnecessary alarm in the kindly old gentleman's breast? But the sinking of the barge seemed highly suspicious, following, as it did, so soon after the fire in the opera box. Not for the first time Simon wished that Dr. Field were at hand to advise him. It seemed more and more plain that the doctor must have stumbled on some piece of the Hanoverian plot and been put out of the way.

As Simon climbed the steps of Number Eight, Rose Alley, he saw Dido's wan face pressed to the windowpane. He wondered if she had been there all day, and gave her a reassuring smile and wave. She darted out to intercept him in the hall.

"Have you got the mish? Come in here—Ma's got a gentleman visitor in the kitchen and Pa's asleep." She pulled him into her untidy bedroom.

"It's all right," Simon said. "My friend's making you a dress and she'll have it finished by tomorrow night. So all you have to do is get cleaned up—you can't wear a new blue merino dress looking like that."

"New blue merino!" breathed Dido, round-eyed. "Coo, I'll wash and wash and *wash!* But what about the mint sauce? Wasn't it dear?"

"No, because my friend had the stuff given to her as a present."

"New stuff and she give it away to someone she didn't even know? She must be loose in the basket!" Such generosity seemed hardly conceivable to Dido.

"Shall I tell your Ma about the dress?"

"Best not jist now. She's been out all day visiting Aunt Minbo at Hampton Court and come home as cross as brimstone! She said I wasn't to disturb her while the gentleman man visitor was there or she'd clobber me."

"All right, I'll tell her in the morning. Good night, brat," said Simon. Hampton Court! he thought. Could there be some connection between this visit and the wreck of the barge?

On his way upstairs he happened to glance back just in time to see Mrs. Twite's visitor come quietly out of the kitchen.

It was Mr. Buckle, the tutor.

"There must be a connection between Battersea Castle and this house," Simon said to himself positively as he got into bed. "And it's time something was done about that load of Pictclobbers in the cellar. I'll go to Bow Street and inform the constables tomorrow."

He wondered what would happen to the Twite family then. Presumably Mr. and Mrs. Twite would be haled off to jail. What would become of Dido? Surely children did not get imprisoned for the misdoings of their parents? Would the poor little thing have to go and live with one of her disagreeable aunts?

Recalling the new dress and the Fair, he resolved to put off his visit to Bow Street until Monday. Let Dido have her one day of pleasure. "After all," he thought, "a day's delay can't make much odds."

He went to sleep.

9

The dinner that the Duke of Battersea gave Dr. Furneaux's students was long remembered at the Academy of Art. As the Duke explained apologetically, the menu was put together at such short notice that the guests could only expect pot luck; just a neatish meal. There were but three courses: the first consisted of oysters, lobsters, salmon, turtle soup, and some haunches of turbot; this was followed by turkeys, chickens, a side of beef, and a whole roast pig; the last course consisted of veal-and-ham pies, venison pasties, salads, vegetables, jellies, creams, and fruit. "Just a picnic," as the Duke observed, "but as we are all such near neighbors I hope you won't take offense that we haven't been able to do better in the time."

Neither Dr. Furneaux nor his students showed any tendency to take offense. The students, many of whom had never seen so much food in their lives before, ate like famished wolves. Gus, sitting by Simon, and surrounded by high ramparts of oyster shells, had eaten steadily and in silence for an hour when at last he broke off to announce with a sigh, "It's no use; I couldn't cram in another crumb, not if you was to pay me. It *does* seem a waste with all that's left! Ah well, this dinner ought to do me for a week, then it's back to apple peel and Mrs. Gropp's parsley. I must say, his Grace is a prime host, ain't he, Fothers? Nothing behindhand about this setout, is there?"

Fothers could not reply; he had eaten nineteen jellies and was leaning back in his chair with a glazed expression.

The Duke stood up and cleared his throat rather shyly, amid shouts of "Three cheers for his Grace!" "Silence for the Dook!" "Pray hush for old Batters!"

"Gentlemen," the Duke said. "My wife and I are very happy to welcome you here tonight. You saved our lives yesterday and we shan't forget it. There has always been a bond between my family and the Academy of Art ever since it was founded by Marius Rivière who, as you may know, married my aunt, Lady Helen Bayswater. From now on the bond will be even closer. I should like to make this dinner an annual event"—("Hooroar for Battersea!" "Good health to old Strawberry Leaves!")—"and I am also going to endow the academy with five scholarships for needy and deserving students. They will be known as the Thames Rescue Bursaries. The first two have already been awarded by myself and Dr. Furneaux in consultation, to Mr. Augustus Smallacombe and to Mr. Simon—I'm afraid I don't know your last name," the Duke ended, breaking off and looking apologetically at Simon, who was so astonished that he stammered, "M-mine, your G-grace? I don't know it either."

"Were you never christened?" asked his Grace, much interested, "or had your parents no surname?"

"Why, you see, sir, I was an orphan," Simon explained. "I never knew my parents."

"Then where—" The Duke's further question was interrupted by Jabwing the footman, who chanced to drop a very large silver tureen full of oyster shells with a resounding crash just behind his Grace's chair. Then the students began cheering Gus and Simon so vociferously that no more could be said. The Duke, smilingly nodding to Simon and indicating that he would very much like to hear his history on a later occasion, stood up and invited his guests to come and view the restored Rivière canvas.

They all trooped up the great flight of stairs from the banqueting hall to the library. Here the end wall had been curtained off by a large piece of material—was it the Duchess's tapestry turned back to front? Simon rather thought so—and when everybody had been marshaled in, and Dr. Furneaux shoved to a position of honor at the front, the Duchess pulled a string to unveil the picture.

The material fell to the ground and there followed a silence of astonishment.

"Devil take it!" exclaimed his Grace. "What's become of the picture? Scrimshaw, Jabwing, Midwink—where's the Rivière gone?"

Nobody knew. "It was there this morning, your Grace," Jabwing said.

"Well, I know that, stupid! You didn't take it out for a last cleanup, did you, my boy?" the Duke asked

Simon, who shook his head.

The Duchess, feeling that the spirits of the party might be sadly lowered by this mishap, cried, "Oh, do not regard it, William! 'Tis odds but it's merely been mislaid and will turn up directly if we do but keep our heads. Let us think no more about it, but, instead, amuse ourselves and our guests with dancing or diversions which I'm sure the young people would much prefer."

"Let's play Hunt the Picture!" exclaimed Gus.

"Capital notion!" shouted somebody else.

"Huzza for Gus!"

"We'll find the picture for your Graces, never fear!"

In a trice the high-spirited students had scattered from the library and were darting upstairs and downstairs, along galleries, through suites, in and out of closets, saloons, antechambers, armories, falconries, heronries, butleries, and pantries all over Battersea Castle in search of the missing picture. They turned the whole place topsy-turvy in their enthusiasm, but the Rivière canvas was not forthcoming, though innumerable other pictures were whisked down from the walls and submitted for the Duke's inspection.

"Is this it, your Grace?"

"Is this?"

"Is this?" Pictures were soon piled high in the library.

But the Duke shook his head to all of them.

"Dear me," sighed the Duchess, "I could wish that these *delightful* young people were a little less *volatile.*"

At that moment a chandelier, on which Fothers had

been swinging from side to side as he examined some pictures that hung rather high up, fell to the floor with a loud crash. The chandelier was shattered but Fothers was unhurt, though he looked rather green.

"Dashed uneasy motion," he murmured. "Like on board ship. Shan't try *that* again."

He picked himself up and went off to search in the muniment rooms.

"Oh, fol-de-rol, my dove," said the Duke, "I don't know when I've enjoyed myself so much. Never seen the old place looking so lively. Anway we won't trouble our heads any longer about the picture—of a certainty some poor half-witted niddlenoll must have gone off with it—one of those whatd'ye-callems with a mad craving for pictures. I'll tell the magistrates about it tomorrow and ten to one the feller will be laid by the heels in a couple of days if he doesn't walk in with it saying he's Henry the Eighth."

Soon after this Simon took his leave, expressing warm gratitude to the Duke and Duchess for their hospitality and for the unexpected and most welcome Thames Rescue Bursary. It was nearly time for his appointment with Sophie.

As he ran down the stairs—matters were in such chaos all over the castle, with students dashing hither and thither, that no footman attempted to see him out—he thought he heard somebody trying to attract his notice.

"Hey there, you! Hilloo! Psst!"

He looked round the hallway and saw Justin waving to him from behind a suit of armor.

"What is it?" Simon said.

"I'm coming to the Fair with you tomorrow."

"Famous," said Simon. "I told his Grace about it and he doesn't mind."

"That ain't to the purpose," Justin said. "I tell you, Uncle Bill's always agreeable. It's Buckle who'd put a spoke in the wheel—sour old cheesebox—but it's the luckiest thing in the world, he's been called away to Deptford on two days' urgent private business—rich aunt dying or some such humdudgeon—and won't be back till tomorrow evening. Where shall I meet you?"

"On Chelsea Bridge, an hour after noon," Simon suggested.

"Tooralooral," Justin said conspiratorially, and disappeared back behind the suit of armor as if he expected that the very walls would report on his plans to Mr. Buckle.

Sophie, true to her word, had finished the blue dress.

"Soph, you're the kindest good girl in the world," Simon said, and gave her a hug. "I'll buy some fairings tomorrow, see if I don't. Now, shall I take you back to the castle?"

"No, for Mrs. Cobb's invited me to stop the night here, thank you."

As Simon had half expected, Dido was lurking up in his room, on tenterhooks with anticipation.

"Have you got it? Have you got it?" she demanded in a whisper before he was through the door. When he lit a candle and showed her the dress she was absolutely dumbstruck with admiration.

"Oh!" she breathed. She took it reverently from him, laid it out on the bed, and stroked it as if it had been a living thing. "*Oh!* Ain't it *naffy!* Shall I put it on now?" She held it up against her.

"Certainly not," said Simon firmly. "If you did, it's odds but you'd go to bed in it and come out tomorrow looking like a piece of mousetrap. You'd best leave it here, where it won't get dropped and trampled on—*I* know how you treat your things."

"I *never* would with *this!* Oh, wouldn't Penny be green if she could see it! I wish I could see her face."

"Well, run along now, cully," Simon said. "The sooner you go to sleep, the sooner morning will come."

She started toward the door, then turned and, coming back, pulled his head down to her level. "Thank you," she whispered gruffly in his ear, then bolted from the room.

But Simon, getting into bed, felt a pang of dismay. Did Dido but know it, she had little cause to thank him for what he was going to do soon.

They set off for the Fair next day in high fettle, met Justin on the bridge, as arranged, and went on to collect Sophie from the Cobbs. Dido was delighted to meet the kitten again there and begged that it might be allowed to accompany them to the Fair, but Simon felt that this would be too much of an anxiety; he had enough responsibility as it was. At first Justin and Dido were inclined to regard one another with jealous suspicion and hostility: Justin looked down on Dido as a gutter brat, and she sneered at him as a high-nosed counter coxcomb. But Simon and Sophie were so cheerful and good-natured that no one could be long in their company without succumbing to their influence and soon the whole party were in charity with one another and marched off toward Clapham in good spirits. Dido thanked Sophie very prettily for the blue dress, while Justin went so far as to say that she looked quite well in it and he wouldn't have recognized her.

The Fair was already in full swing when they reached Clapham Common. Hucksters were shouting their wares, shrill music from the trumpets and hurdy-gurdies competed with them, and the roar of the happy crowds could be heard above that of the giddy-go-round.

"What shall we do first?" said Simon, surveying the colorful booths. "Shooting Gallery, Imperial Theatre showing Panoramas from History, Fat Lady, Snake Charmer, Living Skeleton, Mermaid, Flying Boats, Wise Pig, Drury Lane Drama, Swan Boats on the Long Pond, Whirligigs?"

"Oh!" cried Dido, "everything! *Everything!*"

Simon looked at Sophie. Her cheeks were pink and her eyes shone bright with excitement. "Isn't this famous!" she said. "Who'd have thought, a year ago, that we'd ever be having such a gay time?"

They did everything. They won coconuts at the coconut shies, looked at the Fat Lady and the Living Skeleton (very poor show for a penny, Dido considered), flew on the flying boats (Justin turned very pale, but recovered himself after partaking of seven ginger nuts and a glass of lemonade), and sampled the Drury Lane Drama and the Imperial

Theatre. They interviewed the Talking Pig, which would answer any question put to it—and found that the answers consisted of grunts. They ate oysters and plum cake and ginger wine at Barney's Restaurant. Justin treated Dido to two rides on the giddy-go-round (the Duke had given him half a guinea and he had forgotten to return Simon's half crown); they whirled off, riding on a golden goose and a scarlet camel respectively. Simon took Sophie sailing in a swan boat, and the whole party met again at the shooting gallery, where Simon, whose marksmanship was excellent after several years of hunting for his dinner with a bow and arrow, knocked down ten bottles with ten shots.

"First prize, sir," said the man glumly, and handed Simon a huge china vase. It was so big that Dido could have climbed inside it.

"He doesn't want to carry that about," said the quick-witted Sophie. "Give him what it's worth instead."

The showman gave Simon ten shillings ("I daresay it's worth three times as much" muttered Justin) and he spent it on doughnuts for the whole party and a visit to the fire-breathing dragon (where Dido disgraced them by tiptoeing around to the back and discovering a little man in the dragon's stomach producing jets of steam by means of a boiling kettle).

Then they listened to a lady singing "Cherry Ripe," and inspected the Mysterious Minnikins, who proved to be puppets.

Then, feeling somewhat tired and hungry, they ate mutton pies and drank pineapple punch at a chop stall by the Amazing Arcade, where there were little tables set out on the grass.

By now evening had come and fireworks from the Spectacular Pyrotechnical Display were making wonderful swoops and sparkles and whirls of color against the darkening sky.

"I suppose we should be going soon," Simon said. "Mrs. Twite said Be back by ten, and so did the Duke."

Justin and Dido immediately broke into pleading for "just one more show." "Look, there's a fortuneteller, Madam Lolla," said Dido, "we ain't been to her yet. Oh, *please,* Simon!"

Simon counted his money and reckoned that he had just enough for the fortuneteller and the journey home, so they entered Madam Lolla's booth.

She was a fat, dark gypsy woman with black eyes and a pronounced mustache, impressively dressed in a quantity of purple draperies.

"Cross my hand with silver, young ladies and gentleman," she said affably, and told them that Simon would have a long journey over water, that Justin would soon meet a long-lost relative, and that Sophie would be lucky all her life "because of your pretty face and taking ways, my dearie."

"Pho, what dull, mingy fortunes," cried Dido. "Tell mine! I'll lay there's something more exciting than *that* in it!"

She stuck out her grubby hand to the gypsy, who pored

over it for a minute and then looked at her oddly.

"What's the score, then, missis?" Dido said. "Doesn't I get a fortune?"

"Yes, of course, dearie," the gypsy said quickly. "You'll meet a tall dark stranger and have a surprise and go on a journey."

"Oh, what stuff." Dido was impatient. "Nothing else?"

"Only one other thing," the gypsy said. "You had a present today, didn't you, missy?"

"Yes I did." Dido glanced down proudly at her dress, which, contrary to her usual habit, she had contrived to keep clean and unspotted through all the hurly-burly of the Fair.

"Well, soon you'll be *giving* a present," said the gypsy. "You'll be giving it to the two people as gave you yours, and it'll be a gift as costs you all you've got to give, and is worth more than they know. And there'll be sorrow in the gift as well as happiness but they'll be grateful to you for it as long as they live."

"Is that all? Pooh, what a capsy, weevilly fortune. Give a present, indeed! I'd like to know how, when I ain't got any mint sauce. Nothing more?"

"No," snapped the gypsy, suddenly and unaccountably angry. "You've tired me out, the lot of you. Be off, and leave me in peace."

They were all tired, they realized now. Justin stayed with the two girls under a tree at the Common's edge, watching the fireworks, while Simon ran off and found a hackney carriage. They drove home in the silence of exhaustion, first to the Cobbs, to drop Sophie who was staying there for her week's holiday, and then on to Battersea Castle. Justin wanted to be left at the entrance to the tunnel, but Simon, who had promised the Duke to look after his nephew carefully, thought it best to take him to the main door.

"Ain't this swish?" Dido kept murmuring as they bowled up the long drive between the gas flares.

"Oh, odds boddikins," muttered Justin uneasily as they pulled up. A tall figure stood on the castle steps awaiting them with folded arms.

"It's Uncle Buckle!" exclaimed Dido. She put down the window on her side and called out, "Hilloo, Uncle Buckle! Look at me! Ain't I the dandy? We've been to the Fair!"

"Dido!" exclaimed Mr. Buckle, thunderstruck. He then turned to Justin, who was just alighting, and said terribly, "My Lord Bakerloo! What is the meaning of this—this *escapade?"*

"Uncle Bill said I might go," Justin mumbled sulkily.

"I am sure he had no idea you would be consorting with such l*ow vulgar* companions as these."

"I ain't low!" Dido called out indignantly, but Mr. Buckle took no further notice of her, and went on rating Justin in a harsh, carrying voice. As there was nothing they could do for the unfortunate boy, and it seemed unkind to listen to his setdown, Simon asked the jarvey to drive on to Southwark, the coach turned, and they continued their journey.

"Poor Justin," said Dido, giggling, as they rumbled

through the dark streets. "I wonder if Uncle Buckle will dust his jacket for him? D'you reckon Ma will give me a trimming for going on the spree with a Dook's nevvy?"

Simon thought it unlikely.

"Anyways," said Dido with a sigh, "I wouldn't care if she did! It's been the best bang-up day of my whole life and I'll never forget it, *never!* Wasn't the Punch and Judy a ripsmasher!" She fell into a silence of recollection.

"I never knew Mr. Buckle was your uncle," Simon remarked presently.

"Lor, yes, he's Ma's brother, but we ain't gentility enough for him, so he don't visit us above once in a blue moon. I'll tell you what, Simon," said Dido, looking carefully around as if to make sure that Mr. Buckle was not riding with them in the hack, "I can't give you a present, like Madam Lolla said, but there's one thing I *can* do for you—and I'd *like* to, as you've give me such a prime good time—I can tell you what happened to Dr. Field!"

Simon was silent with astonishment for a moment or two.

At last he said cautiously, "I *should* like to know that, Dido."

"Well, it was like this," she told him. ("Pa said I was never to mention it to a living soul, or he'd beat me and shut me up in the boot hole, but I don't care!") "You see, Dr. Field used to lodge in our house—"

At this moment the hack turned into Rose Alley and stopped outside Number Eight.

"Why, there's Ma!" cried Dido. "Wait till I tell her what

a famous time I've had. Ma, Ma, we saw the Drury Lane Drama!" She opened the door and tumbled out onto the pavement, eager to relate her day's doings. Mrs. Twite, however, only said, "It's long past your bedtime, child. Come along in at once."

Simon paid off the driver and turned to follow Mrs. Twite. But she seemed to have locked the door behind her, and, as he rattled the latch unavailingly and then rapped the knocker, something dark and soft and suffocating was forced down over his head, and a pair of hands gripped his throat. He struggled and struck out, but other hands pinioned his arms and legs, while the clutch on his throat tightened. A rocket seemed to explode on the back of his head, he crumpled forward onto the steps, and was conscious of nothing more.

10

Simon came to by slow degrees. Once, long ago, he had lain ill of a fever at Gloober's Poor Farm, and had been left, sweating and shivering and delirious, in the granary, where he would probably have died had not Sophie sometimes stolen away from her duties to bring him food and keep him covered with horse blankets.

For some time he thought he was back in the granary. It was dark, but he could smell the same smell of meal and canvas and timber; only one thing puzzled him: a strange regular creak and groaning which seemed to come from all around him; he finally concluded it must be the blood pounding in his feverish head. When he tried to move he found he was quite unable to do so.

"I must be very ill," he thought. "I wish Sophie would come."

But Sophie did not come and soon the fever, or nightmare, whichever it was, had him completely at its mercy. Although he could not move of his own will, yet he found himself rolled from side to side as if by a giant invisible hand, and was soon bruised and aching from head to foot.

"Could I be in a cart?" he wondered. "But no; if I were I should hear the wheels and the horse's hoofs; I must be in the granary and I think I must be going to die." He rolled again, this time over and over; it was as if the floor of the place heaved up, up, up, in a long, tilting swing, and then down, down, down, in the other direction; he rolled and slid, helpless and dizzy. How much of this rolling and battering he endured he did not know; it seemed to go on for an eternity of misery, but at last fever and exhaustion and rough treatment overcame his bruised body and he fainted again.

When next he came to it was because somebody was shining a light very close to his face. He moved his head dazedly, opened his eyes, and quickly shut them again. He could hear low voices close to him.

"Hold the glim nearer this way, sapskull! How can I see what I'm doing?"

"Sapskull yourself! It's not as easy as all that. Here, let me do that and *you* hold the light."

"Not on your Jemima! You'd probably slice his dabs off."

Simon became aware that something was being done to his numb, cramped hands. They had seemed immovably jammed against his sides, but now, suddenly, he heard a snap and they were free. He realized that he had been tied up all this time, and struggled feebly to hoist himself on his elbows.

"Wait a minute, don't be in such a pelter, we ain't unfastened your trotters yet," somebody whispered sharply in his ear. Obediently he relaxed and lay back, curling and uncurling his fingers, which tingled as the blood ran into them.

Now he was shoved into a reclining position and found the neck of a bottle tilted against his mouth; he gulped and choked and spat, as liquid ran down his gullet and over his chin.

"Enough . . ." he muttered weakly, pushing the bottle away. "No more now—later."

The drink (it was prune wine) soon did him good; he opened his eyes and looked about. Close to him, illuminated by the flickering light of a candle, were two familiar faces; after a few seconds he identified them as those of Justin and Dido.

"What the deuce . . . ?" He raised himself feebly and looked into the gloom beyond them, where he saw ramparts of piled sacks and timber. "Where am I? What are you two doing here?"

"*Hush!* Don't make a row. We're in the *Dark Dew.*"

"Here, give him another drink," Justin whispered.

Simon accepted another swig. Meanwhile Dido's words had penetrated his mind and connected with something he remembered hearing Mr. Twite say.

"The dark dew? What do you mean? What is the dark dew?"

"It's a ship, o' course," Dido whispered impatiently. "We're all at sea. Ain't it a spree?"

"A *ship?*"

"Uncle Buckle had you shanghaied and taken on board

her at Deptford because you was getting to be such a nuisance, always poking and asking questions."

"Where are we now?"

"*I* dunno," said Dido, giggling. "The *Dark Dew is* bound for Hanover—Bremen, Pa said (that's where they pick up the Pictclobbers, you know)—but they don't take you there. You get dropped off on an island on the way. Inchmore, it's called; fubsy sort o' name, ain't it?"

"But what about you and Justin—what are *you* doing here?"

"That's the cream of it." Dido giggled again. "O' course I didn't know you was going to be kidnapped, though I been suspicioning that Pa would do summat o' the sort. I jist luckily happened to be looking out o' the window arter we got home from the Fair, to see if you was coming in, and I saw Pa and Captain Dark put a bag over your head. Coo, you didn't half struggle! Pa had to clobber you with the butt of his barker, and then they carried you off feet first. I thought I'd follow after; I've never liked it at home above half. Anyways I was jist going to hop it when His Royal Nibs here came along."

"Justin, you mean? But why? We left you at Battersea."

"Yes, well, I wouldn't stand it," said Justin sulkily. "You heard what a setdown the old grinder was giving me, a body couldn't bear any more of it! He said you was a danger to me and he'd see to it I'd never have a chance to meet you again. After the prime time we'd had, too! So after he'd left me with a lot of Latin lines I thought I'd just show him and I went down to the stables and made one of the grooms saddle me a horse (lucky Waters wasn't about) and rode to Southwark. I thought I'd call for you and we'd go to Drury Lane, just to show old Buckle-and-Thong who was master. But when I got to Rose Alley, there was Dido just smitching off to go to Deptford, and she told me you'd been scrobbled. So we thought we'd come along for the lark. Dido knew where the ship lay—"

"Captain Dark allus comes to us when he's got a ship in," Dido put in knowledgeably. "There's three of 'em—*Dark Dew, Dark Dimity,* and *Dark Diamond.* He runs mixed cargoes to Holland, and brings back arms from Hanover—for the Cause, you know. But, Croopus, we had such a time finding you! We sneaked on board in the dark and hid in the forecastle—Justin nipped into a chest and I squeezed behind the grog barrel—and then when we was out to sea we thought we'd look for you but there was such a storm! All we did was fall over! Justin nearly lobbed his groats—didn't you, Nibs?—and I didn't like it above half."

"Oh, that was a storm, was it?" said Simon, remembering the hours of rolling misery. "I thought I was feverish. How long did it last?"

"Matter o' two days. And then it took us forever to find you, on account you was stowed away down here in the hold."

"I'd have been in a bad way, but for you," Simon said gratefully. "But what's to be done now? Does nobody know you're on board?"

"Not a soul. Ain't it famous? We've been having such a game of hide-and-seek! When Captain Dark comes out o' his cabin, Justin nips in and nobbles his bottle of mountain dew (that's what we been giving you). Then the cook comes out o' the galley—I nips in and grabs a black pudding and a hunk of tack. Fast as the sailors coils up the ropes, we uncoils 'em again. We've been undoing things and unwinding things till they think the ship's betwaddled." Dido was laughing so much that here she was obliged to stop and stick the candle in a crevice between two planks because she was spilling hot wax over Simon's legs.

"Are you better, Simon?" she asked presently. "If you are, I've got a bang-up plan."

"What's that, brat?"

"We'll *all* play hide-and-seek with the sailors. We'll turn everything in the ship upsy-down, till they're so set about and dumbflustered they don't know which way they're going, and then we'll watch our chance and lock 'em in the roundhouse, and sail the ship back to Deptford ourselves."

While Simon admitted that this was a pleasing plan, he saw snags.

"Can you sail a ship, Dido?"

"I knows the ropes," she said confidently. "Habbut you?"

"Never been in one in my life before," Simon had to admit, which evidently somewhat dashed Dido's high opinion of him. Justin's acquaintance with ships had been limited to trips up the Thames in his uncle's barge, and it was plain he was not a keen sailor; throughout the conversation he had remained pale and silent, swallowing frequently.

"I don't really believe we can sail the ship ourselves," Simon said.

"Well then"—Dido refused to be cast down—"we'll smidge some barkers—I knows where they keeps the guns and balls—and hold 'em up, make *them* sail us back."

"That's a likelier plan. How many are there in the crew?"

"Matter o' fourteen or fifteen, and most of 'em tipple-topped or right down half-seas-over all the time; Captain Dark's the wust of 'em, you never see him but he's got a bottle in his hand and one in his pocket."

"That's what we'll do, then," said Simon. "Where do they keep the guns?"

"Up on deck, in the roundhouse. We could snibble up now, it's nighttime and there's only a couple of coves on peep-go."

Unfortunately Simon discovered when he tried to move that he was still a great deal too weak to stand. His legs gave way and he fell back groaning against the meal sacks.

"It's no good, brat," he gasped. "I'll have to wait till I get my strength up. Lying tied up all this time without food has left me as limp as a herring."

Dido knit her brows. "I'll lay you'd do better in the air," she said. "This here hold's got a breath in it like a moldy coffin. Let's put him on a sack and haul him out, Justin."

Justin looked doubtful, but when she ordered him not to squat there gaping like a jobberknoll but to find an empty sack he nodded palely and obeyed. They laid the sack by Simon and he dragged himself onto it.

The whole project seemed utterly impossible, but somehow, thanks to Dido's indomitable spirit, it succeeded; Simon was drawn along on the sack to the foot of the ladder that led up from the hold; then, with Dido pulling from above and Justin pushing from below, he contrived to hoist himself up through the hatchway.

"All rug now?" said Dido after a period of rest. "Come on, we'd best bustle or it'll be morning before we're up top."

Once more they set to hauling Simon along a dark gallery. While they were resting in the shadows at the foot of the next ladder, a man came down it, but he never saw them; he reeled as he walked and a strong flavor of spirits wafted from him.

"He's bosky," Dido said calmly. "Drunk as a wheelbarrow. They're all like that—slacking the cables after the storm."

With a fearful effort, Simon was hoisted up the last ladder. Dido's shrimplike frame seemed to possess amazing strength, both in muscle and will power: she hauled like a horsebreaker and exhorted her two companions in a wild flow of whispered gutter language that had a most stimulating effect. Even so, they were all collapsing from exhaustion by the time they reached the deck, and had to lie down helplessly for many minutes. Luckily, as Dido had said, the crew had all been drinking freely after the storm; most of them were asleep and the two on watch were in no state to notice anything unusual.

"Brush on, cullies," whispered Dido presently. "There's a fire in the galley. We might as well have a warm-up, and we're out o' view there."

The galley was a warm and cluttered place; it seemed to serve the purpose of a handy storehouse, for it contained chests and bales and piles of sailcloth. A fire glowed red in an iron stove, and a snoring man lay sprawled on the floor in front of it.

Simon's last recollection was of being thrust into a sort of cocoon composed of rope-yarn and old rags, behind some chests. Then Dido dropped a duffel cloak over him and he slept.

He was roused by a violent blow on the head and opened his eyes with a gasp, thinking that they were discovered. He saw the scared faces of Dido and Justin, who were wedged with him behind the chests; then he realized that they were not under attack; a heavy iron hook, hanging from a coil of rope on the wall, had swung out and struck him. The ship was plunging violently. The hook flew out again, and Simon reached up dizzily and pulled it down.

"We must be running into another storm," he whispered.

The ship echoed and re-echoed with noises—the confused shouts of half-tipsy men, the hum, sometimes rising to a wail, of wind in the rigging, and the roar and crash of the sea itself. They could feel the *Dark Dew* shudder, shrink, and then plunge on as each wave struck her. Feet pattered across the deck and someone shouted an order to reef all sails; the sleeper in front of the galley fire groaned, pulled himself together, and staggered out.

"I might as well prig some peck while the going's good," Dido said, and crawled out from their hiding place. She came back in a moment with two large handfuls of raisins. "There you are, cullies. Keep swallowing, it's much the best in this sort o' toss-up."

"I can't *stand* it," moaned Justin. Dido eyed him scornfully. A dim gray morning light was filtering in through the open door and Simon could see that Dido was as white as a sheet, but she seemed to be alert and cocky, thoroughly enjoying the adventure.

"You *are* a loblolly," she told Justin. "*I* think it's prime—I've never had such a bang-up lark, except for the Fair. I'd sooner be here than at home any day."

"If only the ship wouldn't lurch about so!" whimpered Justin, as a weight of water struck the roof above them with a thunderous crash. "There's water coming in now."

"Pooh," said Dido, pale but game. "That's only a bit of sea hitting the deck."

"But I've got a pain in my breadbasket."

"So've I, but I don't make such a song and dance about it."

"Hush—listen," said Simon, who had been straining his ears. He had caught a long-drawn-out call, repeated twice, and was trying to make it out, as it echoed again over the sound of the wind.

". . . Ay-ay-ay-ay . . . ire . . . ire . . . *Fire!*"

"Fire in the hold! Fire!"

"Fire?" breathed Dido, staring at Simon with dilated eyes. Now she did seem a little scared. "Fire in the hold? But that's where *you* were, Simon! Croopus, it's lucky we got you away from there!"

"That candle, Dido—that candle you stuck between two planks. Did you ever go back and fetch it—or put it out?"

"I—I don't reckon as how I did," she whispered. "D'you think that's what started the fire?"

"It might be."

"Oh, they'll easily put it out," Justin said, hopefully. "Won't they? *Won't* they?"

The other two did not answer. They were listening. A sudden puff of smoke blew through the galley door. The clamor on deck increased, and above the sound of wind and waves Simon now thought he could detect a different noise—could it be the crackle of fire?

"What'll happen?" whispered Dido, very subdued.

"Oh, there must be some boats—if they can't put the fire out—" His words were interrupted by a sudden extraordinary noise, so loud that it seemed to reduce all the sounds that had preceded it to mere taps and whispers. It was a rending, grinding roar that lasted for as long as Simon could draw five breaths—then the ship seemed to stop dead in her course and there was an awesome silence.

"What is it, what's that noise?" cried Dido. None of them could bear to stay in hiding any longer; they all leaped from their nook and ran to the galley door. Simon almost fell from weakness, but grabbed the doorpost and hung on, looking out. Dido clutched hold of his hand.

The scene before them made even Simon gasp. The *Dark Dew,* burning like a torch, had literally broken in half, and the forward part of the ship was already drifting away, carried by the fierce wind and waves. They saw two or three men on it trying to launch a boat; then the whole hulk fell over sideways, swamping boat, crew, and all; in a few minutes it had disappeared from view.

The after half of the ship, containing the galley, remained motionless but continued to burn; great detached fragments of smoke and flame flew past on the wind.

"Wh-what's h-happ-pened? Why aren't we moving?" said Dido with chattering teeth. "D-do you think we've run, ag-ground?"

"On a rock, maybe—" Simon stepped out onto the dangerously canted deck and grabbed at a shroud to steady himself. "Look, there are rocks over there, you can see the waves breaking on them."

"Are we near land?" Dido asked hopefully. "Can we get ashore?"

"Heaven knows. Look, they're trying to get another boat free."

A knot of men at the stern were struggling to drag loose a dinghy that had become wedged beneath a fallen spar. They were in a panic, each cursing his mates and getting in the way of the rest. A wild-eyed man with a black beard rushed past the galley and began knocking the men aside with a wooden spike so as to come at the boat himself, shouting orders meanwhile.

"That's Captain Dark," Dido said. "I'd best go and speak to him, I reckon; we don't want to get left here in the nitch, if they're shoving off."

The boat was freed, now, and she darted across the deck and grabbed Captain Dark's arm. He gave a tremendous start at sight of her, and the rest of the men gaped, thunderstruck at this apparition.

"How do, Captain Dark; ain't this a turn-up, then?" said Dido, pale but perky.

"Where in the name of Judas did you come from, you devil's brat?"

"I ain't a devil's brat! You know me, I'm Dido Twite. I stowed on your ship, with Justin there, acos you was taking my cully away."

Captain Dark turned and saw Justin and Simon; he gave them an ugly glance, and the men by the boat began to mutter, "No wonder we come to this, with a brood of Jonahs aboard. Everbody knows childer bring ill-luck at sea."

Suddenly a great piece of the deck fell in, and flames burst out of the galley window.

"Never mind talking now, skipper! For Godsake let's get the boat launched," someone shouted urgently. Captain Dark shook off Dido and rapped out an order; the boat shot off the deck into the sea. Instantly the whole group of men tumbled off the *Dark Dew* into her, higgledy-piggledy, fighting each other like furies; Captain Dark was among them, wielding an oar vigorously. It was plain there was not going to be room in the boat for everybody. Several men were knocked into the sea but did their best to clamber in again, dragging out their mates as they did so.

"Wait, wait!" Dido called frantically. "Wait for us! You've left us behind!"

"You weren't asked on board, were you?" someone shouted. "Save yourselves, we don't want you."

The boat drifted away. Its crew were too busy struggling for places to worry about pulling at the oars or steering. Simon saw a huge green hill of sea rise beneath its keel and tip the boat sideways like a walnut shell. He could not bear to look any longer and turned his eyes away.

"*Save us!*" whispered Dido in horror, staring past him. "They've *gone! Simon!* They've gone! What'll we do?"

"We'll have to manage for ourselves, that's all," Simon said, pulling himself together, trying to sound more hopeful than he felt.

They clambered down to the stern, which the fire had not yet reached, and then realized what had happened to the ship. Her rudder had caught and jammed between two rocks, so that she was held fast and battered until her forward part had broken away.

"She won't last here long," Simon said. "We'd best shift off as soon as we can. I believe that might be an island over there."

Day had now fully broken and a wild yellow light shone fitfully between squalls of rain. They glimpsed a long, craggy ridge of land about half a mile ahead; then black cloud came down and blotted out the view.

"H-how c-can we g-get there?" asked Justin.

Simon cast his eyes around what remained of the deck. There was a large watercask lashed to the mast; he dragged it free.

"Here you are," he said to Justin. "This'll do for you, neat as ninepence. Pass this bit of rope round your middle and through the bunghole—so—now the cask can't float away from you. Here's an oar; hang on to the end of it and we'll let you down; you can go first as you're a Duke's nevvy."

He rolled the barrel into the sea and Justin, whimpering a little, was let down into it and pushed off with the oar, which Simon then passed to him.

"Fend yourself off from the rocks!" he shouted as the cask bobbed away.

"What about us?" asked Dido, doggedly clenching her teeth. "I can't swim."

Simon looked around once more. There were no other barrels, and the flames were coming uncomfortably close.

"It'll have to be this for you and me," he said, and laid hold of the broken spar which had hindered the men from launching the boat. Ropes were still made fast to it, and he passed a couple of these around Dido and tied her on as securely as he could.

"I d-don't like this above half," she said, shivering.

"Never mind. I'm going to push you in and then jump after you. Hold tight to the pole! Now jump!"

"Oh, my lovely new dress! It'll get ru—"

A wave closed over Dido, but she reappeared next minute, gamely clinging to the spar. Simon dived in and managed to grab the other end of it.

"That's the ticket! Now all we have to do is swim to shore."

"Can you see Justin?"

"Yes, he's floating on ahead of us. We'll be all right; you'll see," Simon said as reassuringly as he could. He gave Dido an encouraging smile and she smiled wanly back. She looked a piteous sight with her wet hair hanging in rats' tails over her face.

Simon swam with his legs, pushing the cumbersome spar ahead of him with his arms. It was an exhausting struggle. His heart grew so heavy in his chest, and beat so hard, that he began to feel as if it would work loose and sink from him like a stone.

"Are you all right, brat?" he gasped.

She made some indistinguishable reply. Presently he heard her say, "Are we nearly there?"

"Just keep going. Kick with your legs."

They labored on. Dido, looking back, cried out that the *Dark Dew* had gone! She had crumbled together like a burning ember and slipped under the waves.

"Lucky for us we weren't on board then," panted Simon. "And I should have been, Dido, if you hadn't come and set me loose. I owe you my life."

"But s'posing it was us that set fire to the ship?" Dido gulped miserably.

"Oh—as to that—very likely it wasn't. With all those drunk men on board, it's a wonder the ship lasted as long as she did."

A wave slopped against Simon's chin and he closed his mouth. He was beginning to feel very strange: his legs were numb from the waist down and hung heavily in the water.

"I—I'll have to stop for a minute, Dido," he said hoarsely. One of his hands slipped off the spar and he only just succeeded in grabbing it again.

"There's a rock, let's make for it," she said. "We can rest for a bit."

With a last effort Simon swam toward the rock. They managed to drag themselves up its slope, getting badly scraped by limpets, and lay side by side on the narrow tip, shivering and exhausted.

"Can you see Justin—or the land?" Dido asked after a while. She huddled closer to Simon. He opened his eyes with an effort, and moved his head, but could see nothing save cloud and driving rain. His eyelids flickered and closed again; he sank into a sort of dream, only half aware of Dido, who occasionally moved or coughed beside him.

Once or twice he realized that she was pushing food into his mouth—damp and salty raisins or crumbs of cheese.

"Keep some for yourself, brat," he muttered weakly.

"I ain't hungry . . ."

In Simon's feverish fancy the rock seemed to sway up and down as the *Dark Dew* had done—tilting, tilting, now this way, now that . . . Or was he on the branch of a tree, back at home in the Forest of Willoughby? Was that sound not the howl of the sea but the howl of wolves? No, it was the sea, but Dido was talking about wolves in the forest; her words came dreamily, in disjointed snatches:

"Climbing from one tree to the next . . . I'd have liked that . . . Shying sticks and stones at the wolves down below . . . you could laugh at 'em . . . it must have been prime. *I* wouldn't 'a wanted to go to London, dunno why you did. You *will* take me there some day, won't you? To the forest? You said you would. And I'll throw stones at the wolves . . . I'm glad you came to London, Simon. Nobody ever told me such tales afore . . . and you took me to the Fair . . . coo, that dragon was a proper take-in, though, wasn't it . . . I liked the Talking Pig best . . ."

She coughed, and crept closer still against Simon. For some time there was silence, except for the harsh screams of gulls. Simon drifted further and further away toward the frontiers of unconsciousness.

"Simon," Dido said presently in a small voice. His only response was a faint movement of his head.

"Simon, I think the tide's coming in. It's coming higher up the rock. I—I don't think there's going to be room here for both of us. Maybe—maybe I'd better try and float to the shore to get help?"

Simon did not answer. His eyes were closed, and he lay limp, white, and motionless, with the waves breaking not three feet below him.

11

Sophie was puzzled. She had been staying at the Cobbs' for five days now, during which time Simon had not once come to see her or to work in Mr. Cobb's yard. Mr. Cobb was puzzled too.

"Simon's sich a reg'lar-working cove in the usual way. I hope there's nowt amiss," he muttered, looking with knit brows at the panel of a barouche which Simon had been in process of adorning with a viscount's coat-of-arms. "Here's thisyer job promised to Lord Thingumbob for Toosday, and looks like I'll be obleeged to cry rope, which ain't my way. I hope the boy's all right. Hey, Sophie, lass! How about your taking a hack—here's a crown for the fare—and tooling round to Southwark to see if he's sick abed?"

Sophie agreed with alacrity and was about to fetch her bonnet when a small grubby boy sidled into Mr. Cobb's yard and made his way toward her.

"Is you Miss Sophie?" he asked, fixing her with a piercing eye.

"Yes I am," she replied. "What can I do for you?"

"You're sure as how you're Miss Sophie? Cos I wasn't to give it to no one else, and, Croopus, I've had sich a time finding you. Fust I axes at the castle—nobody gammons—nearly gets chucked in a horse trough for me trouble. Then a gaffer says to come here. *Is* she Miss Sophie?" he demanded of Mr. Cobb.

"Miss Sophie she be," Mr. Cobb answered heartily.

"Then I can give it you." He handed her a very dirty folded bit of paper, and added hopefully, "She says as you was very kind and 'ud likely give me a farden. And, please, I cooden come afore today, my Gammy's *that* strict I cooden give her the slip, but today she's laid up with a proud toe."

Sophie laughed at this and gave him sixpence, saying, "Thank you, my dear. Here you are, then; buy yourself some Banbury Cakes. But who told you to come?"

He looked conspiratorially around the yard, sank his voice to a whisper, and said, "Why, *she* done. Young Dido Twite. But she's gorn now—along o' the others." Then he bolted off between the carriages and vanished out of the gate.

Sophie opened the note which was addressed, in staggering capitals, to MIZ SOPHY.

Dere Miz Sophy. i thankx yu onst agin fer the dress. its reel Prime. Fust nue dress i iver wuz giv. Simon as bin kid naped in a Shipp. Me an Justin is goin 2 for the Lark. i like Simon an it isn Fare he shd be All Alone. the Shipp is the dark due. Yrs respckfly Dido Twite.

"Good gracious!" exclaimed Sophie, when she had read this letter twice. "He has been kidnapped! And Justin too! Can this be true? I must inform her Grace!"

"*Kidnapped?* Young Simon?" Mr. Cobb fairly gaped at her.

"Yes, on board a ship called the *Dark Due*. Do you know of such a vessel?"

"By Ringo, yes! She and a couple of others belong to that shifty, havey-cavey Nathaniel Dark, the one who ran off with Buckle's wife."

"Mr. Buckle? Justin's tutor? I didn't know he'd ever been married," said Sophie, momentarily diverted from her worry.

"It was years ago. Buckle was glad to be rid of the woman. By all I hear she never stopped talking. Dear knows what Nat Dark did with her, for he didn't marry her; left her in furrin parts, I daresay. He's a dicey cove; up to the teeth with the Hanoverians, too. That settles it," said Mr. Cobb, grabbing his hat from a mounting-block and cramming it on his head. "I'm for Bow Street. Young Simon said summat once about Hanoverians—"

"The Twites, in Rose Alley," said Sophie, nodding.

"Ah, and I said, Leave well alone. But when it comes to kidnapping— It's as plain as a pike what's happened: he's twigged their lay and been put away."

"But where will they have taken him?"

"Ah, there, lass, now you're asking. Those Dark ships goes coasting all the way up to Newcassel and then across to Hanover—they might put him anywhere that's okkud to get at. Only thing is to nobble the bunch—at Rose Alley, you say?—and winch 'em tight till they let's on where he's to. I'll be off to Bow Street."

Mr. Cobb started for the gate, then paused to ask, "Was you wishful to see me, Jem?"

"Only to ask was his Grace's curricle ready yet, Mr. Cobb?" said Jem, coming out from behind a pile of wheels.

"Ready this evening, tell Mr. Waters." Jem nodded and followed Mr. Cobb into the street, where he set off at a run toward the castle.

Sophie was not long in following him. Inquiring for their Graces, however, she learned that they were calling on his Majesty. Not surprisingly, the castle was in an uproar over the disappearance of Lord Bakerloo, and the Duke had gone to ask that a national proclamation be made offering a reward for information as to the whereabouts of the Battersea heir.

Sophie found the Duchess's embroidery (which was suffering from a week's neglect) and sat putting it to rights in the library, waiting for their Graces to return.

The whole chamber was still stacked high with the piles of pictures which the academy students had taken down during their vain hunt for the Rivière. There had been no time to rehang them in the more urgent search for Justin. Sophie, established with her embroidery on a footstool by the fire, was screened by a pile of canvases from the view of anybody entering the room.

Presently she heard two people speaking in low tones.

"This has put a pretty crimp in our plan," a voice said

angrily. "What was that fool, Dark, about not to notice he'd two other brats on board? And *Justin,* of all people—it couldn't be worse." Sophie recognized Midwink's tones.

"What I'll do to that boy when I catch him!" The other speaker was Mr. Buckle. "The whole thing nearly in our hands and he has to run off like a—like a guttersnipe! If those students hadn't been on the riverbank the other day—or if that meddlesome girl hadn't gone to the opera—Justin would have been Duke of Battersea by now and we'd be in clover."

"Well, as things are, he's not," said Midwink sourly. "And the old boy's still alive, and till we get Justin back we'd best *keep* him alive; we don't want some cousin stepping in and claiming the dukedom. I've got the poison but I won't use it till Dark brings back the boy."

"I only hope Dark has the sense to do so," Buckle said with a curse. "It drives me wild having to rely on such a nabble-head. And now we've got to shift the ken from Rose Alley—and if Jem doesn't warn Ella before the Bow Street runners get there—"

"Jem's trusty enough," Midwink said. "He took the Duke's fastest chaser—he'll be there by now. Where did you tell Ella to take the stuff?"

Buckle sank his voice to a murmur and Sophie could only catch the words, "vegetable cart." Midwink gave a cackle of laughter and said, "They'll never think of looking *there.* But are you sure no one will blab?"

"I don't believe there's a soul in the castle that's not a Hanoverian to the hilt," Buckle replied. "Barring the girl.

Now, as to my plan. Soon as we hear from Dark that he has Justin safe—if we hear before the mince-pie ceremony—"

"Aha, you mean to poison the Christmas mince pies?"

"No, better than that." Buckle dropped his voice again and Sophie missed the next words. He ended, "all sky-high together—and the wench as well. My heart's in my mouth, now, every time the Duchess looks at her. Why she had to pick *that* one, out of all the paupers at Gloober's . . . I thought she'd died in the woods but it must be—"

"Hush!" said Midwink. "Is that the carriage? Best not be found here."

The two men left the room.

Sophie remained where she was, almost paralyzed by fear and astonishment. So *Buckle* was at the bottom of the plot—Buckle and Midwink! And Jem was with them, and had galloped off to warn the Twites to leave Rose Alley. And every servant in the castle—almost everybody—was a Hanoverian to the hilt. Moreover it was plain that the Duke and Duchess were in grave danger—two attempts at murder had only accidentally failed and a third, somehow connected with mince pies, was merely postponed until Justin's return. Why Justin? Sophie wondered, and then realized that if Justin became the sixth Duke of Battersea, following the murder of his uncle, he would still be so much under his tutor's thumb that Buckle would in fact control all the ducal power and money. Perhaps it was a blessing, then, that Justin had run away.

But meantime how to protect the helpless, elderly Duke and Duchess? The Duke had the greatest respect for

Buckle, and would be most unlikely to believe any accusation against him unless it were backed by positive proof. Perhaps the raid on Rose Alley would provide this; if not, it seemed to Sophie that the best plan would be to get the Duke and Duchess away from Battersea. But how was this to be achieved?

Her thoughts were interrupted by the Duchess, who arrived in a great bustle.

"Ah, there you are, Sophie, dear child! I am so delighted to see you again.

"We are to depart instantly for Chippings—his Majesty very sensibly suggested that that naughty Justin might have run off there for a bit of wolf-hunting. Pack me up a few odds and ends, will you, my dear, just for a night or two—warm things, it will be cold in the North—don't forget the croquet and my water colors. Ah, you have the tapestry, that's right. You are to come, too, of course, so pack for yourself as well. We start as soon as the train is ready."

"The train, ma'am? Won't his Grace be using the coach?"

"No, he thinks a train will be quicker. He has gone to charter it now."

Sophie was thunderstruck. She had never traveled on a train in her life—indeed the nearest station to Chippings was at York, over thirty miles away; for the Duke, who considered trains to be dirty, noisy things, flatly refused to have them running over his land.

Sophie struggled with her conscience. This seemed a heaven-sent opportunity to get their Graces away from trouble, and she was excited at the prospect of the journey, but still it was her duty to mention Dido's letter. She showed it to the Duchess, who read it with astonishment.

"Dido Twite? Who is Dido Twite, my child?"

"Oh, she is a poor little thing that Simon has befriended, the daughter of his landlady."

"But why should Simon have been kidnapped? And why should Justin have gone with him? Depend upon it," said the Duchess, "this will turn out to be nothing but a Banbury story. Is this Dido Twite a truthful little child?"

Sophie was bound to admit that she hardly thought it likely.

"I have it!" declared her Grace. "You say this *Dark Dew* belongs to Captain Nathaniel Dark? Yes, and I remember him—a shifty rogue who tried to sell his Grace a shipment of abominable smuggled prune brandy, watered, my dear, and tasting of tar. His ships put in regularly at the port of Chipping Fishbury—be sure, those naughty boys have begged a sea passage in order to get to Chippings, and if we travel by train, like as not we shall be there before them. Yes, yes, my dear, I will show the note to his Grace, but, depend upon it, that is the solution. Now, run and pack the croquet things, and do not forget the billiard balls and my small harpsichord."

With a clear conscience Sophie ran off to carry out her Grace's wishes. Packing the water colors neatly into a crate with the harpsichord, she remembered that curious remark of Buckle's concerning herself: "Why did she have to pick that one, out of all the paupers at Gloober's—my heart's in my mouth every time the Duchess looks at her." What could he have meant? Sophie's heart began to beat rather fast. Might it be possible that, all the time, she had relations somewhere? But why should Buckle know anything about it? Pray, Sophie, do not be nonsensical, she admonished herself, and knelt to fasten the croquet mallets into their case.

An hour later they set off. The Duke, not very well-informed about trains, was indignant to discover that even when he chartered a special one it would not come to his door, but had to be boarded at the station. However, a pair of carriages transported the party across London with their baggage to the terminus, where a strip of red carpet running the length of the platform, a bowing stationmaster, and porters bearing bouquets and baskets of fruit restored his Grace to good humor.

Sophie learned with joy that neither Buckle nor Midwink were to be of the party. The first six hours of the journey passed peacefully. After a light luncheon they played billiards in the billiard car until the increasing motion of the train, as they entered more hilly country, rendered this occupation too hazardous. The Duke, having nearly spitted his lady with a cue, returned to the saloon coach, sighing that he wished they had Simon with them, for there was nothing in the world he would like so much as a game of chess.

"I can play a little, your Grace," Sophie said. "Simon has been teaching me. But I fear I am only a beginner."

His Grace was delighted, declaring that any opponent was better than none. "For her Grace can't be bothered to learn the moves." Sophie unpacked the glass set from his valise and they played two or three games with great enjoyment, the more so as his Grace won them all. Then, unfortunately, a lurch of the train threw the black glass Queen to the floor and broke off her crown.

The Duke was greatly vexed by this, but the Duchess said placidly, "Do not put yourself in a pucker, my dear. If you recall, I had this set made for your birthday by the old glass-burner in the forest and, depend upon it, he will be able to put her Majesty to rights again. We can call at his hut on the way to Chippings."

"Ay, so we can, my dear," said the Duke. "What a head you have on your shoulders. Old Turveytop can do the business in a twinkling, I daresay."

Sophie became very excited. "Is that old Turveytop the charcoal burner, your Grace? Why, it was he who brought me up! I should dearly like to see the old man again—he was always so kind to me."

"Old Turveytop brought you up, did he? But you are not related to him, child?"

"No, ma'am. He found me in the forest when I was little more than a baby."

"But had you no clothes, child—nothing to indicate where you had come from?"

"Nothing, ma'am, except a little silver chain-bracelet with my name, Sophie, on a shield, and on the other side a kind of picture with tiny writing that was too small for my foster father to read."

"Have you the bracelet yet, my dear?" said the Duchess,

showing the liveliest curiosity. "I should so like to see it. Since we looked at that Rivière picture I have had the strangest feeling . . ."

Sophie's face had clouded at a sad recollection. "When I grew, and the bracelet would not meet round my wrist, my foster father put it away for me, your Grace. I am sure he will have it still—"

"Why did he not give it to you when they took you to the Poor Farm, my child?"

"He was not there at the time," Sophie said miserably. "He was away on the wolds cutting peat when the overseer came and took me away. I have so often wondered if he know what had become of me."

"Could you not write to him?"

"Mrs. Gloober would not allow it."

"Never mind, child, soon you will be able to tell him yourself."

Poor Sophie was to be disappointed, however. Night had come when they reached York, and they were obliged to rack up at an inn rather than undertake the dangerous journey across the wolf-infested wolds in the dark. They set out early next day in a pair of hired carriages, and, after several hours' brisk driving, had reached the outskirts of Chipping Wold, a huge, wild, and desolate tract of country, moorland and forest, which must be traversed before they reached the village of Loose Chippings. Sophie was on her home ground, here; her eyes brightened and she gazed eagerly about, recognizing every tree, rock, and tumbling stream.

"There! There it is," she presently exclaimed. "There is the track leading to my foster father's hut."

The Duke ordered the baggage coach to wait on the turnpike while the party jolted along the rocky track in the smaller open carriage. Soon they were passing among dark trees growing steeply up the sides of a narrow glen, and the driver whipped up his team and laid his musket ready on the box. After about half a mile the track widened, however, and they reached an open, sunny space where stood a small log-and-turf hut.

Sophie could restrain herself no longer. She tumbled out of the carriage, crying, "Turvey, Turvey! Are you there? It's me—Sophie! I've come back!"

The door of the hut opened and a young man came out. Sophie halted in dismay.

"Who—who are you?" she stammered. "Where's Turvey?"

"He's dead, miss."

"*Dead*? But—but he can't be! Who are you—how do you know?"

"I'm his nephew, miss. Yes, they found my uncle dead—it's ten days ago now—lying spitted with an arrow at his own front door."

By this time their Graces had alighted and crossed the clearing. Sophie turned, speechlessly, to the Duchess, with tears streaming down her face, and was enfolded in a warm and comforting embrace.

"There, there, poor child," said her Grace. "There, there, my poor dear."

"Oh, ma'am! Who could have done it?"

"Eh, it's a puzzle, isn't it?" exclaimed the Duke. "D'you reckon it could have been thieves?"

"It seems a random rummy thing," said young Turveytop, "for every soul knew Uncle hadn't two bits to rub together. But thieves it must ha' been. The whole hut was ransacked and rummaged clear—every mortal stick and rag the old man possessed had been dragged out and either stolen or burnt. There wasn't a crumb or a button left in the place. Yon's where the bonfire must ha' been."

And he stepped back, revealing a huge, blackened patch of grass behind the hut.

12

Simon opened his eyes with difficulty. He was aware, first, of racking pains in all his joints; then that his head hurt. He moved, and groaned.

"Hush up, then, your Grace, my dearie," a voice exclaimed, just above his head. "Hush up a moment while Nursie changes the bandage and then you'll be all right and tight."

Simon hushed—indeed it was all he could do—and a pair of hands skillfully anointed his head with cool ointment and wound it in bandages. "*That's* better," the voice said, "isn't it now, your Grace? Now old Nursie's going to rub you with oil of lavender to keep off the rheumatics—lucky those jobberknolls brought some on the last shipment or it would have had to be cod-liver oil which, say what you like, is *not* so pleasant."

Without waiting for any reply the hands set to work, pummeling and massaging his aching body until he was ready to gasp with pain. But after a little he became used to the treatment, even found it lulling, and drifted asleep again. When he next woke he felt a great deal better. He raised himself on an elbow and looked about.

He was in a small, wooden, cabin-like room, one wall of which was almost entirely window. The room was neatly and simply furnished and the floor was covered with rush matting. A wood fire in a stone fireplace hissed and gave off green flames from sea wrack; the bunk in which Simon lay was covered with a patchwork quilt.

"I must be dreaming," he muttered.

"Dreaming? Certainly not. Nobody dreams in my nurseries. Get this down you, now, my precious Grace."

A firm arm hoisted him up and a cup was held to his lips. He choked over the drink, which was hot and had a strange, sweet, medicinal taste.

"What is it?"

"What is it? he asks. Doesn't know Nursie's own Saloop when he gets it! Best goat's milk, best Barbados (since those robbers won't bring me cane), best orris. You'll sleep easy after that, your Grace, lovey."

While she straightened his pillows Simon for the first time succeeded in getting a look at the person who called herself Nursie. She was a plump, elderly woman, enveloped in a white starched apron. She had a cheerful, rather silly face, and a quantity of gray-brown hair which she wore in an untidy bun on top of her head.

"Where's Dido?" Simon suddenly asked.

"Di-do-diddely-oh. Where's Dido? he asks, and well he may. Where indeed, for there's nobody of that name on *this* island, to my certain knowledge."

Simon's heart sank. "It is an island, then? Are there others?"

"No, my ducky diamond."

"Where did you find me?"

"Out there," she said, and lifted him so that he could see the sea. "We had a tiddely breath of a blow, yesterday, and when the clouds lifted a bit, Nursie looks out and what does she see? A lump of seaweed on a rock, she sees—only the seaweed has arms and legs and there never was seaweed on that rock before—so Nursie gets out the rowing boat and rows across to have a look. And there's his blessed Grace lying up to the knees in water—another half-hour with the tide coming in and you'd ha' been gulls' meat."

"Indeed I am very grateful," said Simon faintly, "but wasn't there also a little girl called Dido, wearing a blue dress?"

"No, dearie," she said quietly.

"I must go out and look for her—and Justin too—" Simon exclaimed, struggling up. A spell of giddiness took him. With a disapproving cluck, Nursie laid him down again.

"Don't you worry your gracious head, my dearie. If the little girl's come to land, Nursie will know soon enough. The island's not so big. Why, there's only—"

Her words were interrupted by a timid knock at the door. She started.

"Well, there! Perhaps the boy *wasn't* dreaming. Unless it's the Hermit."

The door opened and a damp, miserable figure tottered

in: Justin, with his soaked clothes in rags and his draggled hair dripping over a cut on his forehead.

"Fancy!" said Nursie. "If it isn't another of 'em. Well, you *are* a drowned pickle, to be sure!"

"Justin!" said Simon eagerly. "Have you seen Dido?"

"Oh, hilloo, Simon, are you there?"

Justin sank limply onto a wooden settle by the fire. "Dido? No, I've not seen her." He added listlessly, "I dare-say she's drowned, if she hasn't turned up. *I* was, nearly. That wretched barrel broke on a rock. I think you might have found me something better."

His words were muffled, for Nursie had seized a large towel, enveloped his head in it, and was rubbing his hair dry. No sooner had she finished, and combed the hair back from his face, than she let out a shriek.

"Justin! My own precious poppet! My little long-lost lamb! My bonny little bouncing blue-eyed babby!"

She hugged Justin again and again.

"Hey!" protested Justin. "Who do you think you are? *I* ain't your blue-eyed babby—I'm Lord Bakerloo!"

"Oh no you ain't, my bubsy! You can't fool someone as has dandled you on her knee a thousand times. Why, I'd know that scar on your chin anywhere—that was where your pa dropped you in the fender—Eustace was always clumsy-handed—let alone you're as like him when he was young as two peas in a pod. And there's the mole on your neck and the bump on your nose. You're my own little Justin that I haven't seen since you was two years old."

"I'm not, I tell you! I'm Lord Bakerloo!"

"Dearie, you can't be," she said calmly. "*He's* Lord Bakerloo—him over there on the bunk—or the Dook o' Battersea if his uncle ain't living yet. How do I know? Because o' the Battersea tuft—I found it on the back of his head, plain as plain, when I was bandaging that nasty great cut he's got."

Battersea tuft? What did the woman mean? Was she mad? Simon put his hand up to his bandaged head in perplexity, and winced as he touched a tender spot. What tuft?

"You must be dicked in the nob," Justin persisted. "Who are you, anyway?"

"Who am I, my precious? Why, I'm your own ma, Dolly Buckle, that's who I am, and you're my precious little Justin Sebastian Buckle! Where's your pa, then, all these years, what's he a-doing now? I'll lay *he's* feathered his nest. Always a cold, cunning schemer was Eustace Buckle, planning on next Sunday's joint before this one was fairly into the oven."

"B-b-buckle?" stammered Justin. "You're trying to tell me he's my *father?* Oh, what a piece of stuff! I *won't* believe it! My father was Lord Henry Bayswater."

"Oh, no, he wasn't, dearie. And don't speak like that of Eustace. A good husband he may not have been, but a careful father he *was*. It was on account of that that I felt free to go off with Nat Dark (ah, and a snake in the grass *he* turned out to be, dumping me on this island because he said I talked too much). Oh, no, Master Henry Bayswater wasn't your father—who should know better than I, as dandled his lordship on my knee? He had two children, Master Henry did, or so I did hear, off in them Hanoverian parts, two children, a boy and a girl. You," she said to Simon, "you must be the boy, my precious lordship. What's your name?"

"Simon," he told her weakly.

"Simon? O' course it would be—after your dear Ma. Simone, she was, Simone Rivière, Lady Helen Bayswater's daughter, and own cousin to her husband."

"*What?* You mean I'm—But why should I—Oh, no, it can't be true," said Simon, sinking back on his pillow.

"Of course it isn't true!" exclaimed Justin angrily.

Nursie, or Mrs. Buckle, gave them a placid smile. "You'll allow I ought to know," she said. "I as is ma to one of you, and was nurserymaid in the castle when t'other one's Pa was a boy, until the black day I married Eustace Buckle."

"But I don't understand," Simon said. "If this mix-up happened—which I still can't believe—how did it come about?"

"Why, dearie, it's plain as plain. It's all along o' that scheming, artful Buckle. Always off on some plot or ploy, he was, leaving me lonesome with the babby. One time he goes off to Hanover. Well, my lad, thinks I, *I'm* off this time, too, so I goes on a cruise with Nat Dark."

"Leaving *me?*" exclaimed Justin in a voice squeaky with indignation. "Your own *child?*"

"Well, I couldn't take you on a ship, dearie. Puny little thing you were in those days. I left you in good care—with your Pa's sister Twite. Ah, I never did care for that shovel-faced Ella Twite," she added reflectively.

"So what happened?" Simon asked.

"Why, Nat Dark took a sudden dislike to me, dropped me on this island, and here I've been ever since. But what I'd guess happened to you is that Buckle got charge of Master Henry's children somehow—"

"Lord Henry died," Simon put in. "He and his wife both died in the Hanoverian wars." It seemed strange to think he might be speaking of his own parents.

"Eh, the poor young things! That'll be it, then. Buckle took the children, managed to cast 'em off somewhere (the hard-hearted villain, *I'd* tell him what I thought of him) and handed his own babby over to his Grace at Chippings Castle. But what happened to your sister, I wonder?" she said to Simon.

"I think I can guess."

"That Buckle, he's a deep one," she pursued. "Didn't he ever *tell* you he was your own father?" she asked Justin.

"No." Justin looked sick, as if, against his own wishes, he found himself forced to believe the story.

"I'll lay he would have when you got to be Duke. *Then* he'd have been in the driver's seat. Eh, would you ever believe such wickedness? Now I daresay you can do with a bite to eat, and you too, your lordship."

She bustled about, and presently fed them on ham and eggs.

"Mrs. Buckle," said Simon presently.

"Yes, my lovey? (Call me Nursie, do, it sounds so comfortable.)"

"Nursie, if Captain Dark left you on this island, what, fourteen years ago, how have you managed to live?"

"Eh, bless you, love, Nat Dark calls by from time to time on his way to Hanover, with a load of flour, or a pig, or a couple of pullets. I'll say this for him, he's a considerate rogue. But he always lies half a mile offshore and floats the things in on a raft for fear I'd scratch his eyes out if I caught him."

"I see," Simon said. He guessed that, once the conspiracy was under way, both Mr. Buckle and Captain Dark would have an interest in keeping the talkative Mrs. Buckle marooned for fear she should spill the beans.

"Is there nobody else on the island?"

"Only one other." Mrs. Buckle began to laugh. "Eh, he's a rum chap, if you like. I call him the Hermit. Captain Dark dropped him with the groceries last summer. I thought he'd be company, but, bless you! he's not one for a chat. Always painting, he is. 'Mrs. Buckle,' he says to me, 'forgive me, but you're interrupting my train of thought.' Eh, well, it takes all sorts to make a world."

Simon was on his feet with excitement. After the meal of ham and eggs he felt much stronger, almost his own self again.

"Where is he? Is he far from here?"

"Bless the lad, no, nubbut up at top of hill. But mind those legs, now, lovey, you're full weak yet—"

Clucking distractedly Mrs. Buckle followed Simon to the door, trying to fling a pea jacket around his shoulders. He hardly noticed. Behind the cabin was a heathery slope, grazed by a few sheep and goats. He ran up it, found it led to another, and that to a third, which ended in a high crag. At the foot of the crag someone had built a small shack—someone was sitting outside it, wrapped in a cloak, sketching.

"Dr. Field!" Simon shouted. "Dr. Field! Dr. Field! It's me—Simon! Oh, Dr. Field, I'm so glad to see you again! I thought I'd never, never find you!"

13

"Bless me," said the Duke, "you mean there was nothing left at all?"

He stepped into the charcoal burner's hut. The door was half off its hinges. Inside, the place was bare; as the man had said, completely ransacked.

"But what about the little gal's bracelet, eh? Have you noticed a small bracelet anywhere, my man?"

"No, sir. Most likely the thieves'll have taken it," said young Turveytop gloomily, but Sophie noticed him dart a sharp glance around the log walls, as if looking for possible hiding places.

"I believe—" she began, and then checked herself.

"Hark—what was that sound?" exclaimed the Duke.

Sophie turned her head, listening, and became very pale. Young Turveytop rushed to the door. The Duke, following, saw him dart across the clearing to where the open carriage stood, with the driver still on the box.

"Mizzle, you fool! Don't you know what that is?" Turveytop shouted at him, and threw himself onto one of the two carriage horses, slashing at the traces with a knife. In a moment he had galloped off down the track; an instant later the driver had followed him on the other horse.

"Hey! Come back! Stop!" shouted the Duke.

"Good gracious! What very extraordinary behavior! Sophie, what can be the meaning of it? Why have they taken our horses?"

Sophie cast a desperate glance around the open clearing. It was in a coign of the valley: on three sides the forest climbed steeply up an almost perpendicular slope. The fourth side, from which the baleful cry proceeded, was the way they had come.

"Sophie, child, why are you looking so anxious? What is the matter?"

"It is wolves, ma'am, and coming this way. We must take refuge in the hut until they are gone by," Sophie said, trying to maintain a calm voice and appearance.

"Wolves? But—*Oh,* those craven wretches!" exclaimed the Duchess.

"'Pon my soul! Have the men just made off and left us in the lurch? I shall write to *The Times* about this!"

"Please, ma'am—your Grace—*please* go into the hut!" Sophie was almost dancing with impatience; she practically pushed their Graces through the narrow doorway. The threatening, eager cry swelled louder and louder.

Sophie cast about for a weapon. The driver had gone off with his musket, but luckily some luggage had been fastened at the rear of the carriage. She seized a bunch of croquet mallets, a bag of billiard balls, and, as an afterthought, the Duchess' embroidery.

"Sophie! Make haste!" the Duchess called anxiously. Sophie ran back to the hut, where the Duke was vainly trying to adjust the broken door.

"Infernal thing!" he muttered. "Dangles kitty-cornerwise—any wolf could nip through the gap. Have you a notion how we could fix it, Sophie my lass? Ah, croquet mallets, that was well thought of—those should keep the brutes at arm's length."

"I think we can block the doorway—if your Grace would not object to my using your embroidery once again?"

"No, no, take it, take it by all means!" the Duchess cried distractedly.

Sophie quickly folded the massive piece of material into three, and hung it over the door hole, pegging it with slivers of wood into chinks in the log walls.

"What about the windows, my child?"

"My foster father made them small and high on purpose," Sophie said. "Ah! here come the wolves—you can hear the patter of their feet on the dead leaves—"

In spite of her calm and confident manner Sophie's heart beat frantically as the terrible howling swelled around the hut; it sounded like a hurricane of wolves. Soon the hut began to shake as wolves dashed themselves against the wooden walls. Sophie trembled for the precariously fastened tapestry, but the Duke, showing unwonted courage and resource, seized a pair of croquet mallets and stood guard behind it. Sometimes a shaggy head or a pair of glaring eyes appeared at the windows, but the Duchess and Sophie pelted these attackers with a vigorous rain of billiard balls until they dropped back again. Once a corner of the tapestry came loose, as a wolf hurtled against it, and the front half of its body thrust into the room, with fangs bared and slavering tongue, but the Duke and Duchess fell upon it simultaneously and belabored it with croquet mallets until it retreated, yelping, and Sophie with desperate haste pegged the curtain back in position.

How long the battle continued it would he hard to say; it seemed an eternity to Sophie—an eternity of darting from point to point, hurling a ball at one window, reaching up with a mallet to thrust back an attacker at another or strike at a paw that had found foothold on the sill. There was never an instant's rest. But at last the wolves, many of them hurt, evidently decided that this quarry was not to be easily captured. The whole pack ran limping off into the forest; Sophie, on tiptoe at the window, saw them disappear down the track the way they had come.

For many minutes longer none of the three in the hut dared to hope that the wolves had gone for good, but they took advantage of the lull to rest; Sophie and the Duke leaned panting against the walls, while the Duchess sat plump down on the floor and fanned herself with the *Instructions for the Game of Billiards.*

"Sophie! Sophie!" she sighed. "I do not know how it can be, but when we are with you we always contrive to run into such adventures!"

"Come, come, Hettie," his Grace said gruffly. "Admit

that the lass always rescues us, too. It's thanks to Sophie we aren't vanishing down the gullets of twenty wolves at this instant. By Jehoshaphat, my child, you're a well-plucked 'un, and with your wits about you, too; you should ha' been a boy! I'd a thousand times sooner have you at my side in a pinch than that whey-faced Justin."

"Thank you, your Grace." Sophie curtsied absently, but her expression was worried. She knew they must not remain in the hut much longer, for the wolves might return, and night was not far distant.

Regardless of the Duchess's little shriek of dismay, she put aside a corner of the tapestry and slipped out of the hut. Many billiard balls were lying on the grass round about, and she hastily gathered up as many as would go into her skirt and passed them in to the Duke.

"Now, your Graces, I am going to run to the main road for help, so do you, pray, peg up the tapestry again, and do not take it down until you hear me call."

"But supposing you meet with a wolf, my child?"

"I'll make him regret the day he was born," Sophie said grimly, taking another croquet mallet from the carriage. She picked up her skirts and ran like the wind. She met with no wolves along the path but to her dismay, as she neared the turnpike, she began to hear a sound of howling and snarling, mixed with terrified whinnies. She collected a number of small rocks into her skirt and went on cautiously.

Coming around a thicket she saw that, although the main body of the wolf pack had evidently gone elsewhere, half a dozen stragglers remained, and were attacking the baggage coach which still stood in the road. The coachman and one of the horses was missing—it was plain that he had followed the example of his cowardly companion and made off. The other three horses, half mad with fright, were rearing and striking out at the wolves with their hooves. Sophie lost no time in coming to their aid.

"Shoo! You brutes!" she shouted in a loud angry voice. "For shame! Leave the poor defenseless horses alone or it will be the worse for you! Attacking them when they are harnessed up, indeed!" and she followed this up with a hail of rocks, several of which, at such close quarters, found their targets and effectually startled and scattered the wolves. Before they could recover, Sophie rushed among them, whirling the croquet mallet around and around, striking first one, then another, until she won her way through to the coach and jumped up on the box. There, to her delight, she found the driver's blunderbuss, which in his fright he had forgotten to take. She discharged it among the wolves, and this completed their rout entirely; they made off at top speed. Sophie was so much amused at the doleful spectacle they presented as they fled that she burst out laughing, and then applied herself to soothing and making much of the three horses, who were sweating and trembling with fear.

After waiting a few moments to make sure the wolves did not return, Sophie mounted the leading horse, unfastened the traces, and made him gallop back along the track. Arriving at the clearing she harnessed him to the light carriage and called to their Graces to come quickly, for the way was clear.

When the Duchess saw that the wolves were indeed gone she embraced Sophie and allowed herself to be assisted into the carriage. The Duke followed, first taking down the tapestry from the doorway, "for," said he, "it's odds but it will be needed to save our lives some other time."

"Now, your Grace," said Sophie, "if you will but sit on the box with the blunderbuss, I've an errand that won't take a moment—"

"Oh, Sophie! *Pray* be careful!"

"It's quite all right, ma'am, I shan't be gone from your view." And indeed, Sophie merely crossed the clearing to a huge hollow oak on the far side, and put her hand into a small cavity halfway up the trunk. She felt about carefully inside, and her face broke into a smile.

"Ah!" she said. "I thought it was possible the thieves might not know about Turvey's hiding place. He never kept his treasures in the hut, for fear of fire."

She drew out a small bundle, wrapped in leather and tightly fastened. Handing it up to the Duchess, she jumped into the carriage and took the blunderbuss from the Duke, who shook up the reins. The affrighted horse needed no urging to leave the clearing, where the odor of wolf was still strong.

The Duchess, meanwhile, was exclaiming over Sophie's find, as she tried to undo the leather fastenings. "Only imagine its still being there. How clever of you to have remembered the place, Sophie dear! And how strange that Turveytop's nephew was not aware of it!"

"*That* wasn't his nephew!" Sophie said scornfully. "Turvey never had a nephew."

"That man was not his nephew? Who was he, then?"

"One of the thieves, I daresay, come back to have another hunt round. That was probably why he was so quick to make off."

"The wretch!" exclaimed his Grace in strong indignation.

As they had now reached the turnpike again, Sophie busied herself with unharnessing the horse and setting him back in the shafts of the baggage coach. This, being enclosed, would be the safer conveyance in which to complete their journey.

Sophie offered to drive, but the Duke, who had been a famous whipster in his youth, pooh-poohed this suggestion, telling her that she had done quite enough fire-eating for the time, and must now sit inside, rest, and prevent her Grace from falling into a fit of the vapors which might afflict her when she reflected on the perils they had passed through.

Her Grace at the moment was far from thinking of vapors; she was still eagerly tugging at the knotted leather thongs of the little packet. "How provokingly tight they are fastened! I am so impatient to see what is inside this little bundle, Sophie dear!"

Sophie, remembering the old man's treasures, watched with rather a sad smile. At last the knots were undone and the contents poured into the Duchess's lap. Her Grace stared at them, somewhat dismayed: instead of gold or jewels they consisted of a knotted root, shaped like a fist, some quartz pebbles, a few dried-up flowers and berries, a stone with a hole in it, and a sprig of white heather.

"But the bracelet?" exclaimed her Grace.

"Here it is, ma'am." And Sophie, with gentle fingers, delved to the bottom of the little heap and brought out something so black and tarnished that it might easily have been thrown away as rubbish.

"Mercy! Is that silver? It does not look like the second-best dinner service," the Duchess said, eyeing it doubtfully.

"Indeed it is silver, ma'am, and when I have polished it with hartshorn and spirits of wine you will be surprised at the difference," Sophie replied briskly, to cover the slight catch in her voice at the thought of the kind old man who had kept her treasure so carefully.

Fortunately both hartshorn and spirits of wine were at hand, since the Duchess never traveled without them, for fear of a faint, so, for the next twenty minutes, while the Duke drove them along at a fast canter, Sophie occupied herself with vigorous polishing.

"Now, ma'am, tell me if it is not much improved," she said at last, and held up a slender shining chain, at the end of which dangled a little shield. The Duchess took it with trembling hands. On one side of the shield the name SOPHIE was engraved; on the other side was a coat of arms between two names so tiny that it was impossible to read them.

"My quizzing-glass—where is it? Quickly, child. Why, that is the Battersea coat of arms!"

"Can you read the names, ma'am?" said Sophie, trembling.

"Wait a minute, wait—I can nearly see—this coach rocks about so—H E N—Hen—what is that next letter, can it be an R? Why yes, Henry! *Henry Bayswater!*" the Duchess read out in an astonished voice. "And *Simone Rivière!* Sophie! My child! My own dear husband's dead brother's long-lost child!"

And she enfolded Sophie in a suffocating embrace.

"But ma'am," Sophie said in a dazed voice. "Do you mean to say—How can this be?"

"Oh," said the Duchess impatiently, "depend upon it, it is somehow the fault of that wretched, careless Buckle. I *thought* it had been said that Henry and Simone had two children, but Buckle, when he came back from Hanover with the baby, swore the girl had died. In reality, I suppose, he lost you in the forest on the way to Chippings and was ashamed to confess. Only fancy, so you are Justin's sister! I declare, you look a thousand times more like the family than he does. No wonder I have always felt so drawn to you. No wonder you resemble the girl in the picture—she was your mother, Simone."

"Simone?" said Sophie, thinking hard. "That was my mother's name? And she had two children, a boy and a girl? Do you know, ma'am, I believe that Justin is *not* my brother—I believe I know who my brother is—"

The two of them had been so absorbed by their discoveries that they had not noticed the coach draw to a halt.

"Well, my lady," the Duke said, putting his head in at the window, "do you mean to stay there chattering all day, or had you not observed that we've reached Chippings and our good Mrs. Gossidge is waiting to welcome us?"

"But I'm *that* put about, your Graces," declared Mrs. Gossidge, a pleasant, rosy-faced woman, dropping a whole series of curtseys, "for, the weather being so bad, and not knowing your Graces was on the way, I've next to nothing fit to put on the table, bar a singed sheep's head and a dish of chitterlings—but there! I see you've brought Sophie with you, so I daresay she'll turn to and help me, having a light hand with the paste, if she hasn't learnt too many grand London ways."

"Put anything before us that you've got," said his Grace good-humoredly, "for we are devilish sharp-set—your singed sheep's head will do famously. Is Master Justin here?"

"No, your Grace, why, should he be?" Mrs. Gossidge looked bewildered. "Isn't he with your Grace, then? Mogg! Hold the horses still, do! and Sophie, bustle about then, girl! Take up her ladyship's things and then come and help me in the kitchen!"

"Wait a minute, Gossidge, wait—" the Duchess called. "Miss Sophie isn't—William! Only think what we have discovered—"

But Sophie, twinkling at her Grace, had jumped down and run upstairs with a load of knitting wools, while the Duke had hurried off to the stables, and Mrs. Gossidge had vanished to re-singe the sheep's head and get out all her jars of preserved whortleberries.

14

After three days on the island of Inchmore, Justin was a changed boy. He declared that he had never had such prime fun before, that he would like to stay on an island for the rest of his life "out of reach of old Buckle, with his prosings and preachings about the duties of dukes." He added, "I'd sooner have my ma, any day. She's a one-er, ain't she, Simon? And as for being a lord, now I've thought it over I reckon it's a mug's lay; I never liked it above half, and that's the truth. You're welcome to the life, Simon—Buckle and all. I'm only sorry Buckle's my Pa; I'd as lief there was no connection."

Simon thanked Justin absently for his good wishes. The island air did not appear to have done Simon so much good as it had Justin; he was thin and pale, and Mrs. Buckle clucked over him concernedly. He had, in fact, spent most of the three days in a vain search of the island for Dido, assisted by Dr. Field.

"Oh, she'll be as right as a trivet somewhere, I daresay," Justin asserted, and Mrs. Buckle said comfortably, "Now, don't you worry, my dearie. Depend on it, any child of that tight-fisted, stony-hearted Ella Twite will be all right—she'll fall on her feet, you may lay."

But on the afternoon of the fourth day, when Simon was once again scouring the rocky, cliff-fringed beach, he found, washed ashore, the very broken spar with ropes tied to it which he and Dido had used to help them swim to the rock.

Now hope was dead indeed. Simon stood staring at the spar for a long time, as if he expected it to speak and tell him what had happened. Justin, who had come running up to exclaim over it, checked himself, and Dr. Field quietly drew him away; Simon turned and walked off along the shore at top speed as if he hardly knew where he was going.

"Eh, dearie dear!" said Mrs. Buckle distressfully. "Young folks allus takes things so hard. Poor lad. Poor lad. I daresay the little lass was nothing much, wi' those parents—still, I'm sorry I said what I did about Ella Twite. Shouldn't you go after him, Dr. Field?"

"Best leave him to get over it by himself," Dr. Field said, looking after Simon with concern on his kind face.

Simon was gone a long time; he made the complete circuit of the island, and did not return to Mrs. Buckle's until the rising tide and gathering dark warned him that he must delay no longer. It was bitter cold; a few flakes of snow stung against his face and the foam wreaths on the sand were beginning to be crisp with frost.

As he approached Mrs. Buckle's hut, crunching over the

shingle, Justin ran out and caught hold of his arm.

"Hurry, Simon! There's another ship in! Mrs. Buckle says it's *Dark Dimity*—putting in beyond the headland. They've lowered a boat!"

"Ah, there you are, Simon my boy!" Dr. Field was as excited as Justin. "I was about to come in search of you. It's best we all stay together. I daresay the scoundrels want to ask for news of *Dark Dew*. Maybe we can somehow turn this to our advantage. Do you boys hide behind a rock, for they don't know you're here. Mrs. Buckle, come with me."

He strode down to the landing place—a natural rock jetty shelving into deep water—and the boys crouched down in the dusk, listening to the splash of oars.

While they searched for Dido, Dr. Field and Simon had exchanged their stories. Simon learned that, as he had guessed, Dr. Field had overheard the conspirators in Rose Alley discussing a scheme to murder the Duke of Battersea by setting fire to his opera box. Full of indignation, he had rushed impetuously into their midst, shouting, "Traitors! Assassins! Miserable wretches!" and had been outnumbered, overpowered, and haled off to the *Dark Dew,* which happened to be in port at the time.

"I suppose I was lucky to be marooned on Inchmore and not tied into a parcel and dropped into the river off Wapping Stairs," he remarked. "But I should soon have become devilish bored here—the light in winter isn't good for painting. And Mrs. Buckle, kind soul though she is, I find beyond anything tedious. I've been longing for a chat with old Furneaux or a game of chess with the Duke. Only fancy your being his nephew, Simon—though I thought all along you must be related, as soon as I had a sharp look at that Rivière painting. (I'm glad to hear you've cleaned it, by the way.) Bless me—" he burst out laughing, "bless me, what a shock it must have been to Buckle and the Twites when, no sooner had they got rid of me, than you turned up, an orphan from the Poor Farm at Loose Chippings, spit image of Simone Rivière *and* with a gift for painting. Of course they knew I was expecting a boy, but they couldn't have known who you'd turn out to be."

"There's Sophie, too," Simon said. "I hope she's not in dreadful danger. If Buckle realizes—We must get back as soon as we possibly can. Who knows what may be happening while we are here?"

Now the boys could hear the creak of oars in rowlocks, and there came a hail from the boat: "Is that you, Field? Stand where we can see you and keep your arms raised above your head, or you'll get a dose of medicine you don't like and it'll take the form of lead! You too, Mrs. Buckle! We want you to answer some questions."

"Oh, Elijah Murgatroyd!" quavered Mrs. Buckle. "How can you be so wicked, threatening a poor defenseless woman with one o' them horrid guns; put it away, now, do! Guns are never allowed in my nurs—"

"Stow your gab, Dolly Buckle!" the voice said, sounding more human. "Now then, Dr. Field, speak up. Has the *Dark Dew* put in here this week?"

"If we tell you, will you give us a passage to the mainland?"

"Not on your Oliphant! Captain Dark would have my guts for garters if I did."

"No he wouldn't," Dr. Field said calmly. "The *Dark Dew* went down with all hands in the storm three days ago. Burnt out—the crew were drunk at the time—split on a rock, and broke up."

"Is that the truth?" The voice sounded incredulous.

"True as I stand here."

Simon heard a muttered discussion in the dinghy: "Reckon it *could* be the truth, Cap'n Murgatroyd?" "*Could* be—dear knows there's enough liquor and loose screws aboard *Dark Dew*—if it ain't, where in tarnation *is* the brig?" "Dolly Buckle may have thought up this tale." "Maybe; I'm not taking any chances yet, that's suttin. Dr. Field!" the voice went on.

"Well?"

"Have you any remedies for quinsy?"

"Quinsy? I usually give ipecac—" Then the doctor checked himself and asked instead, "Who has quinsy?"

"Two of my men on board have it, mortal bad."

"You'd best let me look at them," Dr. Field said, while in the same breath Mrs. Buckle cried, "Beef tea, beaten egg in hot milk, and cocoa! Oh, the poor fellows, lying sick on that nasty ship without a woman's care! Let me aboard to nurse 'em, Elijah, do!"

Captain Murgatroyd and his mate conferred in low tones. Presently Murgatroyd said, "No harm if you come aboard for the night, I suppose. We was going to heave-to till tomorrow anyway. But no nonsense, mind! You're not coming away with us. Dolly Buckle can make a quart or so o' beef tea and cocoa, and that'll last the men till they're better."

"I'd best dose you all while I'm at it," Dr. Field said. "Quinsy is highly infectious. I'll have to get my medicines."

One of the men accompanied Dr. Field, the other assisted Mrs. Buckle to carry eggs, goat's milk, and spirits of rhubarb to the dinghy. Presently it pulled away with its cargo and the two boys stole back to Mrs. Buckle's hut and settled down for the night, Justin to sleep peacefully, Simon to toss and turn in wakeful misery, thinking of Sophie and Dido.

Early next morning he rose and looked out. A thin snow was falling and beginning to lie on heather and rocks. *Dark Dimity* was still anchored in the bay, and a dinghy was pulling toward the shore. Unsurprised, he saw that its sole occupant was Dr. Field. Simon woke Justin and the two boys ran to the jetty.

"Doped the lot of 'em," said Dr. Field, grinning cheerfully as he shipped his oars and indicated two men sprawled on the bottom boards. "They're all sleeping like babies. Help me get these beauties ashore and then we'll go back for some more."

"How did you do it?" Simon asked.

"A species of seaweed that's common on the rocks here is a powerful soporific. I ate some myself one month, when Dark was a bit slow bringing the groceries; put me into a deep sleep for two days; Mrs. Buckle thought I'd stuck my spoon in the wall. Woke up feeling fit as a fiddle, though. So I dried and powdered a lot; thought it would come in useful if ever I got back into practice. Yes, that's right, drag them into the hut."

"Won't they be surprised to wake up and find we've gone off and left 'em!" giggled Justin, delighted at the neatness and simplicity of the plan. He helped Simon ferry over the rest of *Dark Dimity's* crew, two by two, with a few supplies. ("We must be humane, after all," Dr. Field said. "We'll tell the Preventives about them when we land, and they can come and fetch 'em to jail.")

Mrs. Buckle meanwhile, scandalized at the disreputable condition of the ship, had been scrubbing decks and polishing brasswork; she would even have attempted to wash and mend the dirty, ragged sails, had there been any soap, and had not Dr. Field dissuaded her.

"There'll be work enough sailing the ship to land," he warned her. "I've kept the two men with quinsy; they're still too weak to give trouble. They can take it in turns steering while the boys and I handle the sails, if you'll keep guard over them with a gun, Mrs. Buckle."

"What, me touch one o' them nasty things? I'd as lief blow me head off!"

But when she found it was not loaded and was to be used merely as a threat, Mrs. Buckle agreed. The *Dark Dimity,* being on the return journey from Hanover, was loaded down to her marks with pistols, Pictclobbers, gunpowder, and bullets.

The two sufferers from quinsy quailed at the sight of

Mrs. Buckle nervously waving a blunderbuss, and were only too anxious to obey Dr. Field's orders, the more so when he told them they should go free if the *Dark Dimity* arrived safely at the port of Chipping Fishbury.

Shortly after noon the *Dark Dimity* weighed anchor, with one of the two invalids steering while Dr. Field and the boys worked the capstan. As the brig left the shelter of the island her sails slowly filled with wind. They had all been too busy to notice the weather, but now Simon realized that it was snowing fast; the flakes streamed past him in ribbons of white, blown by a knife-edged wind from the northeast; when he looked back, presently, from his perch in the rigging (for they had already found it necessary to reef some sails) he saw that Inchmore was no more than a white bump amid the threatening waves.

"It's a good thing we built up the fire before we left," Dr. Field said. "Those men are going to be feeling cold by the time they wake up. This wind is exactly what we need; we can run before it all the way to Chipping Fishbury."

He rubbed his hands in satisfaction, stamping his feet on the snow-covered deck to warm them. "Mrs. Buckle! I don't think those two men will give any trouble now. How about putting your blunderbuss away and going to the galley to make us all some of your excellent hot beef-tea?"

15

A huge fire blazed cheerfully in the nobly proportioned fireplace of Chippings Castle great hall. Beside it the Duchess dozed in an oak settle, surrounded by her embroidery. Occasionally she woke and put a stitch or two into the tapestry.

Upstairs, in an attic leading onto the castle battlements, the Duke was happily occupied with one of his experiments, something to do with air balloons. After the last few weeks of excitement, rescues by land and water, perils of fire, drowning, and wolves, not to mention the loss of a nephew and the discovery of an unexpected niece, his Grace was badly in need of peace and solitude.

Sophie, seated at the fireside opposite the Duchess, also appeared to be peacefully engaged—in mending the Duke's socks—but her thoughts were not peaceful. She was anxious and miserable, longing to be back in London. The party had now been at Chippings for three weeks, but still Justin had not turned up. Everybody here was kind and faithful, she was sure, and the Duke and Duchess were safe, but Sophie felt dreadfully isolated. She wanted to know what had happened in Rose Alley. What had become of Simon, Justin, and Dido?

It had been snowing now for two days, there were reports that the wolves on the wolds were becoming very bold, and Sophie feared greatly that the castle might be cut off from all news for weeks and weeks—perhaps until spring.

As if to give emphasis to her thoughts, a baleful howling arose outside, and the stabled horses neighed and stamped in fear. Sophie shivered, threw a log on the fire, and went to look out of the window, but although it was hardly more than midafternoon the day was so dim with whirling snow that she could see nothing.

The Duchess nodded, yawned, and opened her eyes. "What was that noise, Sophie dear?"

"I'm afraid it was wolves, ma'am."

"Oh dear me, wolves so early? I suppose that means we shall not be getting the evening paper from York," her Grace said dolefully. But just then they heard a fusillade of shots, a tremendous jingling of sleigh bells, and, almost immediately, an urgent tattoo of knocks upon the great door of the castle.

Sophie ran to the door, but old Mogg the steward was before her.

"All right, all right," he grumbled, letting down the massive bars. "Leave a bit of t'door standing, cansta? We doesn't want t'wolves taborin' in and setting by her Grace's fire—"

"And we don't want the wolves biting off our breeches pockets while you fiddle with the bolt!" shouted an impatient voice.

"Naay, that's nivver t'paper boy?" muttered Mogg, scratching his head. "Happen t'wolves got him and yon's t'replacement? Or could it be woon o' they doddy travelin' salesmen? Ye can coom in, but coom in slow and careful, for if ye're a highwayman I'll shoot ye full o' gravel chips," he warned, and pulled an ancient pistol out of his green baize apron pocket. He stepped back from the door, which burst open, allowing four people and a wolf to surge into the hall. The wolf was chased out again, with kicks and curses; Sophie gave a joyful shriek.

"*Simon!* You're *safe!* Oh, how glad I am to see you. And Justin too!—their Graces will be so relieved. Ma'am, ma'am, see who's here!"

"What about the evening paper?" grumbled Mogg, but nobody heeded him amid the cries of wonder, relief, and joy. Sophie was hugging Simon, the Duchess was simultaneously patting Justin's head and shaking hands with Dr. Field, though rather puzzled as to how he came to be with the party.

"Why, if that beant Dolly Buckle!" old Mogg suddenly ejaculated. "Eh, Dolly, my lass, 'tis a rare long year since we've seen thee here! Wheer's 'a bin, lass?" Then his jaw dropped and he gaped at Simon, whom he had only just noticed. "And who's *thon?* Why, t'lad's the dead spit of Mester Henry as died in Hanover!"

"Who is he?" shrilled Mrs. Buckle. "Who is he? Why, use your wits, Matthew Mogg, who should he be but his young lordship?"

"Nay," said Mogg obstinately, "*yon's* his young lordship, Mester Justin there, nobbut skin and gristle, granted, but he's bahn to be lordship for all that."

"Him? He's my Justin that I never thought I'd rear, aren't you, my lovey?"

Justin looked slightly embarrassed and sidled away from his mother's embrace. "But as for Master Simon," she went on, "he's family, not a doubt of it, for he's got the Battersea tuft."

"Tuft, sitha? Let's see, then, lad. Kneel down on t' flagstones, tha be's such a beanpole." Rather puzzled, Simon submitted to the old man's parting the thick black locks on the back of his head, where Mogg evidently found what he expected, for he cried, "Eh, tha's reet, Dolly, my woman! To think that I should see the day! Eh, your Grace, tak' a look at this!"

"Why, what a curious thing!" the Duchess remarked. "A little tuft of white hair among the black, precisely like the one my husband had before all his hair turned white. Is that the Battersea tuft?"

"Indeed it is, ma'am," Mrs. Buckle cried. "All the Battersea babies have had it."

"Then Sophie must have it too—Sophie, child, kneel down!"

Sophie, laughing, allowed Mrs. Buckle to uncoil the

curls of her long dark hair and discover the little white tuft on the back of her head. "I never knew it was there myself!" she said.

The Duchess was looking from Simon to Sophie and back, declaring in wonder, "I do not believe I have any eyes at all! Why did I never notice the likeness before? Of course they are brother and sister! Why, they are as like as one guinea to another. We must tell his Grace the news at once!"

"He's in the attic," Sophie said, and she ran from the room. As she darted up the winding stairs she wondered what troubles Simon had been through, to make him look so pale and haggard. She had asked where Dido was, and he had answered, "I can't tell you here," in an undertone, and with a look that went to her heart. Poor Simon! Poor Dido! What could have become of her?

Sophie knocked on the attic door and ran into his Grace's workroom, which was full of a general mess of scientific apparatus lying strewn over several large tables. The Duke was not there, but the outer door onto the battlements was open and gusts of snow were blowing in.

"Your Grace? Uncle William?" Sophie called. "Are you there?" She peered through the open door into the snowy dark. A lighted lantern stood on the leads, and there were footprints in the snow but she did not see the Duke until she looked up.

"Mercy!" she exclaimed.

A pair of legs was dangling just above her. Peering past them through the flutter of snowflakes, Sophie could just see the outline of an extremely large air balloon above her head; it was rising and tugging his Grace upward as he clung to it with one hand, while with the other he held on to the guttering of the attic roof.

"*Your Grace!* Oh, pray take care!" Sophie gasped. She pulled at his legs with all her strength, and then, discovering a dangling rope, ran it through a staple evidently intended for mooring, and dragged the balloon and its passenger back to safety.

"Ah, thank you, Sophie, my child," said the Duke, wiping off the snowflakes which had settled on his hair and eyebrows. "I was just wondering how much longer I could hang on. The mooring rope slipped out of my fingers after I had pumped in the gas. Have you made it fast? Capital. Is it not an excellent balloon? I am delighted with my work; quite delighted. It surpasses all my expectations as to buoyancy."

"Yes indeed, it's beautiful," Sophie said, dragging his Grace indoors as if she feared that he, too, might take off into the night air. "Only think, Uncle William, Simon is here!—and Justin, and Dr. Field, and Mrs. Buckle—Simon has the Battersea tuft, which proves he is my brother and your nephew, and Justin is Mrs. Buckle's son—oh, it is all most complicated. And I am sure they have had *such* adventures, do, pray, come and hear all about it!"

The Duke looked quite bewildered by this stream of news, all delivered at top speed, but he permitted Sophie to pull him down the winding stairs and into the great hall.

In no time the whole party was sitting down to crimped

fish, pickled cockles, venison, and whortleberry pies, and a huge platter of spiced parkin. While they ate, Sophie and the Duchess bombarded Simon and Dr. Field with questions, and each told his tale; Mrs. Buckle put in explanations until the whole story of Buckle's plot and the Hanoverian conspiracy was made plain. Sophie then recounted how she had heard Buckle disclose his intentions to poison the Duke as soon as Justin returned.

Justin, who had been looking more and more miserable and apprehensive as the tales were told, revealing him as the unwitting tool of all this villainy, now broke down altogether and fairly boohooed.

"None of it's my fault," he howled. "I never asked to be swapped as a babby, and prosed and preached at and made into a Duke! Oh, boohoo, n-nobody likes me and I shall be t-turned out into the snow to starve! I wish I was back on Inchmore with my ma, I do!"

The Duchess exclaimed warmly, "*Nonsense,* Justin dear, nobody thinks of putting you out in the snow. Nobody blames you for what you didn't know about—I am sure we all pity you for having such a thoroughly unpleasant father. You can go back to Inchmore if you wish, next summer—in winter I am sure it must be most disagreeable and you had best stay here at Chippings with your mother, who has kindly agreed to help Mrs. Gossidge with the housekeeping. Now stop crying and do not be such a great gaby! Mrs. Buckle, perhaps he is overtired and should be put to bed."

"Indeed he should, your Grace, I declare I'm ashamed

of him," exclaimed his mother, and whisked him away, crying, "Come along, my ducky, do, and don't make such a show of yourself, my precious lambkin, or Ma will be obliged to give you two Gregory's powders and a spoonful of calomel. Look at Simon. *He's* not crying!"

Simon looked pale and heavy-eyed, however, as the Duchess noticed with kindly concern. Dr. Field quickly finished the tale of their adventures: they had turned *Dark Dimity* over to the Preventives at Chipping Fishbury, the two recovered sufferers from quinsy had been allowed to ship as deck hands on a collier going south, and, learning that the Duke was at Chippings, the rest of the party had come straight there in a hired sleigh, only slightly hindered by wolves on the way.

The Duke looked quite bewildered at this tale—he always found it hard to take in many new ideas all at once—and as everybody was fatigued with emotion and excitement they decided to go to bed and leave the discussion of plans till next day.

All night the snow fell steadily, and by the morning it lay five feet deep in the castle court, and the drifts were three times the height of a man. From the embrasured windows nothing could be seen but a white wilderness in which the trees seemed to be standing waist-deep. But at dawn a pale sun rose, drawing brilliant sparkles from the icicles on the branches.

"Now," said Dr. Field, who was sitting with the Duke and Duchess at a late breakfast, "We have only two problems."

"What are they?" asked Sophie, pouring his chocolate.

She already felt a great confidence in his practical sense.

"You say that Cobb sent the Bow Street runners round to Rose Alley?"

"Yes, but I fear they will have found nothing. The Twites had been warned by Jem."

"There has been nothing about it in the papers," the Duchess put in.

"Neither Mr. Cobb nor the Bow Street officers knew that Buckle was involved?"

"No, for I overheard him plotting with Midwink *after* Mr. Cobb went to Bow Street."

"So Buckle at present thinks himself secure, and knows nothing of the loss of *Dark Dew* and *Dark Dimity.* Our two problems are to discover where the Hanoverians now keep their arms, and to reach London fast enough to take them by surprise."

"I have a very good notion of where the Hanoverians now put their arms," the Duke said. "Just before we left, Buckle asked me if he might house his fossil collection in Battersea Castle vaults. I said I had no objection, and gave him the key."

"Of course!" exclaimed Sophie. "That's why Midwink said, 'They'll never think of looking there.' You can enter the vaults from the tunnel, can you not? They could move the things in with very little risk of being seen."

"And as for traveling to London," pursued the Duke, "I have the most suitable equipage upstairs that could be devised—a strong, commodious, elegant air balloon, capable of carrying at least eight persons and their luggage for hundreds of miles. Simon, my boy, which way does the wind blow?"

Simon, who had been gazing out of the window, deep in sorrowful reverie, jumped at being addressed, but replied readily enough, "It still blows from the north, your Grace."

"Nothing could be more convenient. I have been working on a steering device for the balloon, but I am not yet fully satisfied with it. A north wind, however, should blow us straight to London."

"Travel in a balloon!" exclaimed the Duchess, aghast. "William! Are you out of your mind? We should all be killed—blow away to the South Pole—starve—freeze to death—crash to the ground—stick in a tree—*oh,* the very idea gives me the vapors!"

"Nonsense, Hettie," said the Duke impatiently, as Sophie administered hartshorn and fanned the palpitating Duchess. "We shall be famously snug. We can take up a brazier to keep us warm, besides fur rugs and such gear, food, amusements, knitting, and so forth; then, if we want to descend, why, we merely pull the cord and slowly deflate the balloon. It's as simple as kiss your hand!"

Dr. Field was delighted at this plan.

"Besides," the Duke pursued, "have you forgotten the mince-pie ceremony on Christmas Eve? It is our loyal duty to be back for that."

"What is the mince-pie ceremony, your Grace?" inquired Dr. Field. "And where does it take place?"

"Why, you see," explained the Duke, "it is the hereditary duty of our family to furnish the King with mince pies, and the presentation always takes place in Battersea Castle on Christmas Eve. In fact we have the King to dinner, serve some mince pies at table, and give him a washbasket of 'em to take away afterwards, while the trumpeters blow a special tune called the Battersea Fanfare. If we start today—it's five days to Christmas—we ought to arrive in nice time for the ceremony."

Sophie, Simon, and Dr. Field looked at one another in dismay. With such a nest of vipers hiding under its roof, Battersea Castle seemed the most dangerous place in the world to invite King James III for a mince-pie dinner. Would there be time to clear out the Hanoverian conspirators beforehand?

"I daresay Buckle knows nothing about this ceremony?" Dr. Field said at last, hopefully.

"Pshaw, my dear fellow, he has made all the arrangements for years. Besides which, I wrote him by carrier pigeon last week, reminding him to have the mince pies baked in good time."

"This complicates matters," said Dr. Field, scratching his head. "As your Grace has pointed out, we must get going at once. We shall need plenty of food, charcoal, telescopes, a weapon or two—"

"Dominoes, playing cards, spilikins, billiard balls," noted Sophie, ticking them off on her fingers, "thank goodness, at least we need not fear wolves in a balloon—"

"But suppose there should be eagles!" cried the Duchess fearfully. "Oh, William! Need we really travel in this dreadful apparatus? I shall be unwell, I *know* I shall be unwell!"

"Smelling salts, hartshorn, spirits of wine," Sophie noted down.

"And, Sophie my dear, whatever else you put in, pray do not forget your Aunt Henrietta's embroidery!"

16

Four days later, on Christmas Eve, the great rose-colored balloon was drifting over the wooded heights of Hampstead.

Sophie, paying little attention to the snow-covered landscape as it passed slowly by beneath, was busily engaged with making a court dress for the Duchess to wear at the mince-pie ceremony; she sat in a whirlpool of apricot-colored velvet, which she was embroidering with topazes. Sometimes the Duke raised his head from the chessboard to say with a chuckle, "Bless me, Sophie, m'dear, it's fortunate that I built the car as big as I did; any smaller and, with all that stuff of yours, some of the passengers would have had to hang over the side!"

In fact, the wicker, galleon-shaped car, with its high-decked ends and low waist, was excellently adapted to their needs. Dr. Field and the Duke played chess at the forecastle end, Simon steered on the poop, directing the balloon's progress, when necessary, by means of a pair of dangling ropes, while Sophie with her dressmaking and the Duchess with her patience occupied the central portion.

One night, when all the others were sleeping, snug under furs and sheepskin rugs, Simon had told Sophie the whole sad story of Dido's end, and his own grief and remorse that he had not been awake to stop her from trying to swim to shore.

"For I am sure that is what happened, and I should have saved her, Sophie."

"You must not think in that way, Simon dear, for it is wrong," Sophie said, affectionately clasping his hands. "You could do no more than you did—Mrs. Buckle has told me how ill you were. And—do you know?—somehow I cannot be sure that Dido is drowned. Somehow I believe that she is not."

"Why, Sophie, what else could have happened?"

"Oh, I do not know—perhaps a ship could have rescued her. I feel in my bones that we shall hear of her again. So do not grieve too much. You did all you could for her and were a deal kinder to her, I am sure, than any of her miserable family."

This talk with Sophie cheered Simon a great deal.

It was decided that, when they reached London, Simon should instantly repair to Chelsea Barracks, to enlist the help of the Yeomanry against the conspirators, while Dr. Field escorted the Duke and Duchess to Battersea Castle.

"For Buckle will scarcely try any of his villainy so long as he remains uncertain of Justin's whereabouts," he pointed out.

Justin had been offered a ride to London in the balloon, but had refused with horror; a sea voyage was quite bad enough, he declared. He was to remain at Loose Chippings with his mother, who would only come to London if it was needful to give evidence against her infamous husband.

"I will tell Dr. Furneaux and the students that we are back, also," Simon suggested. "They are all good fellows who enjoy a fight and, being so close to the castle, they will be handy in case of trouble."

"You could arm them," Sophie observed, biting off a thread (she had completed the Duchess's gown and was now finishing one for herself, white tissue with gold ribbons). "If Uncle William has a spare key to the castle vaults on him, they could let themselves in and take some of the Hanoverians' Pictclobbers."

This sensible plan won instant approval and the spare key was handed to Simon.

The travelers were fortunate in the timing of their arrival over London. Snow had been falling all day, but toward dusk the clouds dispersed, drawing away westward in great high-piled crimson masses across which the balloon drifted south, inconspicuous against such a flaming background.

"We shall be able to take Buckle by surprise," Dr. Field said with satisfaction. "Good heavens," he added, looking down at the snow-covered city of London sprawling beneath them, pink in the sunset glow, "Wolves in Hyde Park already—before Christmas! I fear it is going to be a hard winter. Best prime your pistols, Simon; if they have reached Hyde Park they may have reached Battersea Park; you may have to dash for it."

Soon they saw the Thames, a shining ribbon of ice that curled its way between Chelsea and Lambeth.

"There's Chelsea Hospital," Sophie said.

"Dear me! I had best reduce the pressure." The Duke gave a tug to the string which released the air valve; some air escaped, and the balloon's silken globe sank, crinkling and quivering, until they were barely above the rooftops.

"Oh, William! Pray take care!"

"I know what I am about, my dear," his Grace said testily.

In fact the Duke had misjudged his landing a little, but this turned out to be just as well, for he had proposed to alight in Battersea Park, which was full of wolves. Instead the balloon came to rest in Mr. Cobb's yard, where the proprietor was alone, greasing the runners of a high-perch phaeton sleigh.

"Weel I'll be drawed sideways!" he exclaimed. "If that ain't the neatest rig I ever did see! Simon, me boy! Well, I *am* pleased to see you! We'd given you up for lost, indeed we had—thought the wolves must 'a got you. And his Grace! And her Grace! And little Miss Sophie! Floss!" he bawled up the stairs, "here's our boy Simon back, safe and stout, wi' all the castle gentry! It be a proud day when your Graces sets foot in my yard!"

He helped the Duke and Duchess down, while Mrs. Cobb, and Libby with the kitten in her arms, came marveling out to gaze at the great rose-colored bubble that had settled by their front steps.

"Thank'ee, thank'ee, Cobb, my man," the Duke said. "We should be greatly obliged if you could let us have a conveyance to take us to the castle."

"Why, your Graces can have thisyer phaeton sleigh, it's as sweet a little goer as ever slid, and I've a beautiful pair o' match grays, won't take but a moment to put them to. But that balloon! Dang me if that don't beat cockfighting, that do! I'll soon be in a new line o' business if sich things gets to be all the crack!"

He fetched a pair of horses and harnessed them to the sleigh, while Dr. Field helped the Duke and Duchess to their high-perched seats.

"Mr. Cobb," asked Sophie, climbing up behind them, "did the Bow Street runners find anything when they raided Rose Alley?"

"Nay, lass, the birds had flown. Someone must 'a peached, for never a soul was there, not so much as a grain of gunpowder. There, your Grace, that's all right and tight. Watch for the wolves in the park, sir, they be fair audacious. But these horses can show them a clean pair of heels. Is this gentleman a-going to drive?"

He handed the reins to Dr. Field.

"Much obliged, Cobb, thank'ee. Now, can you do us one more kindness? Can you ride like the wind to Bow Street and ask them to send some brisk, stout officers to the castle—we are expecting trouble, and his Majesty may arrive at any moment. Dear me, yes," the Duke said, inspecting his timepiece, "we must hasten. I hope Buckle has everything in readiness; it was unfortunate that we were blown off course for two days. However I daresay all will be well—Buckle is such a capable fellow—in his way. Simon, my dear boy, we shall hope to see you at the castle directly you have informed Dr. Furneaux and the Yeomanry."

With a creak and a jingle the sleigh sped away.

Mr. Cobb offered Simon a horse, or his own donkey, but he said that he could go faster on foot. He raced down to the academy where, most fortunately, Dr. Furneaux was outside, superintending a snow fight between a dozen of his students on the frozen river, while the rest of them sat on the bank attempting with numb fingers to sketch the scene.

Dr. Furneaux let out a cry of joy at sight of Simon, which, to anybody who did not know him, would have sounded more like a roar of fury.

"*Ah, scélérat, coquin, misérable! Méchant gars! Espèce d'espèce!* How do you dare to show your face, after being absent so many days and giving your poor old teacher so much worry! I will bastinado you, I will escallope you, I will use your head for a doorknob!" He hugged Simon and shook him with equal ferocity.

"It was not my fault, sir, I promise you!" Simon exclaimed, half laughing and half choking as he tried to escape from these signs of affection. "I have had such adventures—And, sir, I have found Dr. Field! He is back in London—he will come to see you very soon! But I must not stop to tell you now. Sir, his Grace the Duke asks a favor of you. He has just returned to Battersea Castle, where there is a nest of Hanoverians. I am going for the Yeomanry, but meanwhile could some of the students station themselves near the castle—just to look out for trouble, you know?"

"*Entendu,* why certainly, nossing could be simpler. *Étudiants!*" roared Dr. Furneaux, "away, all, to Battersea Park, to sketch ze castle against ze sunset!"

"I say, though, dear old sir," pointed out Gus, who stood nearby, "what about the wolves in the park? Know how it is when you're sketching—get absorbed—wolf sneaks up behind—poof, snip, snap, swallow!—and all your paint water's spilt."

"*Vraiment,* zat is a difficulty. Aha! I have it. One student will paint, ze ozzer fight wiss ze wolves."

"Famous notion! But what does he fight with?"

"We know where there are some weapons," Simon interposed, and gave Gus the key to the castle vaults, explaining that the door led to them from the tunnel. "Watch out for Hanoverians, though; they may have somebody on guard."

"We'll clobber 'em if they do," said Gus joyfully.

Simon ran off to Chelsea Barracks with a lighter heart; plainly the students would be prompt to the rescue, should trouble arise in the castle.

Unfortunately he encountered great difficulty in carrying out his mission at the Barracks; they appeared to be deserted, and when at length he did discover an officer (engaged in taking a Turkish bath) he was told that half the regiment had been put to sweeping the snow off

Parliament Square, while the rest were away on Christmas leave. However the officer promised that he would try to get fifty men onto Chelsea Bridge in an hour's time, and with this unsatisfactory arrangement Simon had to be content.

He himself hurried back toward the castle, hoping that Mr. Cobb had been more successful at Bow Street.

As he reached the corner of the King's Road, his ears were assailed by a mournfully familiar music—a sad and breathy tooting which could come, surely, from only one player and one instrument. He looked about, and saw a tall thin man with a luxuriant black beard and mustaches, standing in the gutter and playing on a hoboy. In front of the man lay a cap, with a few coins in it.

"Mr. Twite!" Simon exclaimed.

The man started. "No, no, my dear young feller," he said quickly. "Must be mistaken, somebody else, not that name, Twite? No, no, quite another person."

But the tones were unmistakable in spite of the disguising beard.

"What are you doing here, Mr. Twite?"

The musician glanced quickly up and down the street.

"Well, my dear boy, since you *have* plumbed my incognito—avail myself of the chance of a word with you. Delighted to see you back, by the way—missed you."

Mr. Twite spoke in the most amiable, carefree manner, as if his had not been the hand which, at their last meeting, dealt Simon such a stunning blow. He led Simon into a doorway and went on confidentially, "A tombstone for my wife I will not ask, for between you and me she was a thorn—"

"Tombstone? But—I don't understand." Simon was mystified. "Is Mrs. Twite dead?"

"No," replied her hubsand cryptically. "Not *yet*. But dear little Dido—the last of the House of Twite—the flower of the flock—I should wish that some suitable memorial be erected to her on the island of Inchmore. A simple stone with a simple legend—perhaps *Dido Twite, a Delicate Sprite?*"

"Yes—yes of course," said Simon, somewhat shaken. "But—you heard, then?"

"Those two sailors from *Dark Dimity* whom you so kindly liberated reached London yesterday and told my brother-in-law the whole tale. I'm delighted to hear that my dear young nephew Justin is still in good health."

"But—good heavens—if Buckle knows *that*—then the Duke and Duchess are in deadly danger. I must be off to the castle at once!"

"I most strongly advise you *not* to." Mr. Twite laid a detaining hand on his arm. "No indeed, that is the *last* place I should visit at present. But perhaps you were not aware that Mr. Buckle proposed to blow up their Graces and his Majesty shortly by means of dynamite?"

"*What?*"

"Buckle's somewhat *wholesale* arrangement is that, at nine o'clock, when he himself, and his followers, will have left the place, a lighted fuse will reach the charge in the vaults. The Duke and Duchess and his Majesty, peacefully unaware of their solitude, will be alone in the castle preparing to watch from the library a display of fireworks which they have been told will take place as the clock strikes nine. Fireworks! My brother-in-law is seldom humorous, but that strikes me as a neat touch."

"But if that is so—let me go! I must run. I must warn them! Thank heaven it is only a quarter to five," Simon said, as the church clock's chimes rang out not far away.

"Wait, wait a moment, my rash young friend. To tell the truth," said Mr. Twite, again looking round cautiously, "I have of late become somewhat wearied by my dear wife and her family and their burning political ambitions. I resolved to rid myself of the whole boiling and start afresh, overseas, in a land where musicians are treated with respect. So—in short—I altered the fuse—*cutailed* it—timing it to explode at *five,* when my dear wife, brother-in-law, sisters-in-law, and the rest of them will still be inside the castle. Was not that an ingenious notion? I flatter myself it was," he said, rubbing his hands. "Dear Ella, her sisters, Eustace Buckle, Midwink, Jem, Fibbins, Scrimshaw, and that disagreeable fellow who calls himself young Turveytop—yes indeed, the world will be a more peaceful place without them. Dear me, the boy has not waited! Think, think, my impetuous young friend!" he called after Simon. "Reflect on what you are doing!"

But Simon, his heart pounding in his chest, was racing at top speed toward Mr. Cobb's yard.

17

"Is my coronet on straight, Sophie? Are my gloves properly buttoned? These diamond buttons stick so—"

"Come on, come on, Hettie, there's not time to waste, I can hear the cheers! His Majesty will be here at any moment!"

The Duke took his wife's arm and fairly ran her down the stairs. Sophie and Dr. Field followed protectively near. As yet, nobody had noticed them. The castle servants appeared to be in a state of disorganization, all milling about downstairs; neither Midwink nor Fibbins had appeared to help their Graces.

As they descended, Buckle's voice could be heard below, giving orders to a large number of people: "You all know what you have to do—every soul to be out at half-past eight. After the fanfare and the dinner—disperse! Each carry something: Midwink take charge of the jewels, Scrimshaw the plate—"

"Good evening, Mr. Buckle," the Duke said. "Are the arrangements for his Majesty's reception all complete?"

Buckle whipped around. For an instant an ugly expression came over his face, but this was rapidly replaced by his usual pale-eyed, impassive stare.

"Quite ready, your Grace," he replied smoothly. "I am glad to welcome your Graces back to Battersea."

"Well, you won't be when you hear our news!" the Duke snapped. "We know that you're a damned scoundrel, who palmed off your own whey-faced brat in place of my nephew and niece, and tried to murder me three times! But your crimes have caught up with you, and I shall be surprised if you don't end your days in the Tower, you rogue! The Bow Street men and the Yeomanry are on their way now; we don't want any unpleasant scenes at present, but as soon as his Majesty has left you'll be arrested."

Mr. Buckle's eyes flashed, but he replied in a low, even tone, "Your Grace is mistaken. I intend to amend my ways. I see my faults—I am truly sorry—and in future your Grace will have nothing to complain of."

"Well," said the Duke, a little mollified, "if you are *truly* sorry—"

"William!" exclaimed the scandalized Duchess. "Don't believe a word the hypocrite says! I am sure he has not the least intention—"

"Hark!" interposed Sophie. "Here is his Majesty! I can hear the fanfare, and the students cheering."

Indeed, as the royal sleigh left the frozen Thames, along which it had sped from Hampton Court, and crossed the short snowy stretch of park to the castle, the assembled students burst into loyal shouts.

"Hooray for Jamie Three!"

"Long live King Jim, good luck to him!"

"Yoicks, your Majesty!"

The Duke and Duchess, with Sophie behind them, ran down the red-carpeted front steps of the castle to greet his Majesty while the students formed a ring and, with snow-balls and horse chestnuts, kept the inquisitive wolves from coming too close.

"Sire, this is a happy day. We are so pleased to welcome you to our humble roof—"

"Och, weel, noo, Battersea, it's nice to hear that. And how's your gude lady?"

The King was a little, dapper, elderly Scottish gentle-man, plainly dressed in black, with a shovel hat on top of his snuff-colored wig; he carried a slender hooked cane, and a large black bird perched on his wrist which, at sight of the Duchess, opened its beak and gravely remarked, "What's your wull, my bonny hinny?"

"Mercy on us!" exclaimed her Grace. "Where did your Majesty get that heathen bird?"

"Why, ma'am, the Sultan of Zanzibar gave her to me for a Christmas present. And I find her a great convenience—don't I, Jeannie, my lass?—for there's a wheen Hanoverians aye trying to slip a wee drop of poison into my victuals, so I e'en employ Jeannie as a taster—she takes a nip of brose and a nibble of parritch, and soon has the poisoned meat sorted. Not that I mean to decry your hos-pitality, ma'am, but one must be careful."

"Why yes, yes, indeed one must!" The flustered

Duchess then pulled herself together and graciously invited his Majesty to do himself the trouble of stepping into the banqueting hall. Sophie, following, noticed a pale gleam in Buckle's eyes, and thought he looked as if he meant mischief. She wished the Bow Street runners would come, or the Yeomanry—surely it must be nearly an hour since they parted from Simon? What could have happened? She could see that Dr. Field shared her worry, for he kept glancing at his watch.

"What time is it?" she whispered to him when a dour-faced female (Aunt Tinty, had she but known it) brought in the mince pies, with flaming prune brandy poured all over them.

"Twenty minutes to five," he whispered back. "Where the devil can that boy have got to with the Yeomanry?"

"Will you have a mince pie, your Majesty?"

"Na, na, thank you, Duchess. They play the very deuce with my digestion. But Jeannie will, won't you, lass?"

Jeannie ate several mince pies with every appearance of satisfaction, smacking her beak over the prune brandy.

"Are they safe?" Dr. Field whispered to Sophie.

"I brought them from Chippings," she whispered back. "I wouldn't trust the mince pies Mr. Buckle had provided."

Even so, none of the party save Jeannie felt inclined to sample the mince pies. She, after her fourth, perhaps because of the prune brandy, suddenly became overexcited, flew around the banqueting hall twice, pecked Mr. Buckle on the ear, and disappeared through a small open window.

"Jeannie—come back, lass!" cried her master, starting up. "A gold guinea to the man who catches her!"

None of the footmen seemed moved by this appeal; they stood motionless, and one or two of them sniggered. Sophie felt ready to sink with shame, but Dr. Field went to the window and shouted to the students outside, "His Majesty offers a gold guinea to the person who brings back his pet bird."

A tremendous cheer went up, and the sound of many running feet could be heard, accompanied by cries of hope and disappointment.

"Shall we adjourn to the library for coffee?" the Duke suggested. "I believe later on we are to see some fire-works." The party began moving up the stairs. "I daresay one of the students will soon bring back your bird—" the Duke was going on comfortably, when suddenly the most astonishing hubbub—shouts, shots, and crashes—broke out downstairs by the main doors.

"Gracious heavens!" cried the Duchess in alarm. "What can be going on?"

A somewhat bedraggled Gus burst through the castle doors and came charging up the stairs. His hair stood on end, one eye was blacked, and his face was covered by what looked like peck marks, but he held the squawking Jeannie triumphantly in both hands.

"Here you are, your Majesty!" he panted. "And I wish you joy of her! She's a Tartar! But sir and ma'am, and your Majesty, I don't think you should stay here, I don't indeed. Those villains downstairs are up to tricks, I believe. I had the devil's own job to get in, they were all massed about the hall with pikes and Pictclobbers. The sooner you are all out of the castle, the better it will be, in my opinion."

"Oh dear, oh, William!" lamented the Duchess. "We should never have let his Majesty come here—"

"Nonsense, Hettie. The Yeomanry will be here directly. All we need do is keep calm and retire to the library till it all blows over."

"Let us go higher up! That noise terrifies me—it sounds as if they are all fighting each other before coming up to murder us."

"What does his Majesty say?"

His Majesty had been busy settling Jeannie's ruffled plumes and politely affecting to be unaware of his hosts' problems. Appealed to, he said amiably, "Och, let us go higher up, by all means. Did ye not say there were to be fireworks? The higher up, the better view."

"I winna say nay to a wee dram," remarked Jeannie unexpectedly.

"Hush, ye ill-mannered bird. Lead the way upstairs, then, Battersea."

The Duke had the key to a small privy staircase leading to the battlements, and up this he led the King, while the rest of the party followed.

It was now almost dark, except for a fiery pink streak lying across the western sky; down below in the park the obscurity was broken by flashes as the students skirmished with the wolves and aimed a shot from time to time at Hanoverians in the castle doorway.

"Brave boys! They're keeping the scoundrels boxed in!" exclaimed the Duke. "When the Yeomanry come—oh, why *don't* they come?"

"But look—look who *is* coming!" Sophie pointed, almost stammering in her excitement. "The balloon! It must be Simon!"

"Why does he come in the balloon? Because of the wolves?"

"It is certainly Simon!"

An applauding shout went up from the students as the balloon drifted over them, shining in the light of the gas flambeaux which were now beginning to illuminate the park. Simon leaned over the side and shouted down urgently, "Keep away from the castle! Away, for your lives!"

Then he threw out some ballast, and the balloon soared up to the level of the battlements. Grasping the hooked end of the King's cane, he was drawn close to the castle walls.

"Please, your Graces and your Majesty—don't waste a minute!" he begged. "Climb on board, quick! You are in the most deadly danger—there is not an instant to be lost! Sophie, Gus, Dr. Field—jump in as quick as you can!"

He sprang onto the battlements and helped the Duke lift his wife into the car.

"I say, ain't this a famous balloon, though?" said Gus, helping Sophie. "Will it hold us all, Simon, me boy?"

"Yes, yes—only hurry!" Simon was frantic with impatience as the King somewhat stiffly and gingerly clambered into the waist of the car, assisted by Dr. Field and the Duke.

At this moment Buckle rushed out of the attic door onto the roof, followed by Mrs. Twite.

"I told you they were escaping!" she shrieked, her face distorted with rage. "I told you I saw a balloon! After them, Eustace, quickly!"

Buckle started toward Gus, who felled him with a large snowball and leaped nimbly on board. Mrs. Twite threw herself at Simon and grabbed him around the middle.

"Oh, you wretch!" she exclaimed, pummeling him. "I'll teach you to come meddling, asking questions, helping them to escape just when the Cause is about to triumph!"

"Who the deuce is that harpy?" the Duke asked in bewilderment.

"Simon, quick—dodge her!" Sophie cried anxiously. Everyone else was now on board and the balloon was already moving away from the castle walls in the evening wind. Simon wriggled out of Mrs. Twite's grip, dodged her around some chimney stacks, tripped Buckle, who tried to intercept him, ran for the battlements, and, with a tremendous effort, hurled himself across the rapidly widening gap. He fell sprawling over the gunwale, half in and half out, but Sophie and Gus grabbed him and hauled him to safety. Meanwhile the car tipped and lurched terrifyingly, then sank a few feet. The Duke and Duchess with desperate haste flung overboard all the loose articles of baggage they could lay hands on to lighten the load: braziers, rugs, provision hampers all went tumbling into the park, and the balloon rose higher.

Mrs. Twite let out a fearful shriek of disappointed rage, but Buckle, with an oath, pulled out a pistol and fired at them.

"Mercy, mercy, he's hit the balloon! Oh, what shall we do?" cried the Duchess.

Sophie bit her lip. They could all hear the hiss as air rushed out of the puncture. The balloon started to sag.

"Dear me! Hadn't reckoned on anything like that," muttered the Duke.

"I have it!" cried Sophie suddenly. "The tapestry! Aunt Hettie's embroidery! Simon, can you climb up and lay it over the hole?"

She handed him the bundle of material and he swarmed up a guy rope and flung an end of the cloth over the top of the globe. Gus caught and held it tight on the other side, and the air escape was checked. Dr. Field scrambled to the tiller, to steady their progress, and the balloon glided, swayingly, down and away from the castle.

"Oh, oh, he's going to shoot again!" cried the Duchess.

Buckle, with deadly intent, was aiming at the balloon once more.

But as they watched, frozen in suspense, the thing that Simon had been expecting came to pass. With a noise so loud that it seemed no noise at all, the whole castle suddenly lifted up, burst outwards, and disintegrated in one huge flash of orange-colored light. The balloon rocked and staggered. Fragments of stone showered about them.

The Duchess fainted. Fortunately the hartshorn had not been flung out; Sophie was able to find it and minister to her Grace.

"Dod!" said King James. "Nae wonder ye were in sich a hurry, my lad! We're obleeged to ye—very. Aweel, aweel, that rids the world of a muckle nest of Hanoverians—but I'm afeered there's no' much left of your castle, Battersea."

"No matter, no matter!" said the Duke somewhat distractedly. "To tell truth, I never greatly cared for it. I should much prefer to live at Chippings. We'll lay out a pleasure garden on the site—yes, that will be much better. Simon, my dear boy, I can't thank you sufficiently. We are indebted to you for all our lives. Sire, may I present to you my nephew Simon, Lord Bakerloo. As for those miserable Yeomanry and Bow Street runners, we might as well never have applied to them for all the help they have been."

But as they sank slowly toward the snowy grounds of the academy, a sound of martial music was heard: the banging of drums and squealing of fifes heralded the arrival of the Chelsea Yeomanry who came marching in brave array down the Chelsea Bridge Road, while along the bank of the river twenty Bow Street officers galloped at full speed, led by Mr. Cobb. Meanwhile the students, having observed the balloon's escape, had come running across the park, and all these forces converged to welcome the rescued party as they reached the ground.

Dr. Furneaux was in the forefront.

"Ah, my poor sir, my dear friend!" he exclaimed, giving

the Duke a bristly hug. "How I commiserate wiss you. Your home lost! destructuated by zese brigands! (Not zat I ever admired it, indeed, a most hideous building, but still, ze saying goes, does it not, ze Englishman's castle is his home?) And poor Madame, *hélas!* But nevaire mind, you shall live in ze academie, bose of you, if you wish. I make you most welcome, and my students shall design you a new castle, *moderne, confortable, épouvantable!* Ziss we shall do directly!"

"Oh, thank you, dear Dr. Furneaux, but we think we shall retire to Chippings, and turn the castle grounds into a pleasure garden for you and your students. Meanwhile his Majesty has kindly offered beds at Hampton Court to myself and my wife and niece and nephew here, and Dr. Field."

"Niece and nephew?" Dr. Furneaux stared in bewilderment first at Simon and Sophie, then at the Duke. "What is ziss? What of ze ozzer one—ze little Justin?"

"It was a case of mistaken identity," the Duchess explained kindly. "Simon is our real nephew and heir; he will be the sixth Duke of Battersea."

Dr. Furneaux was aghast. "*Ah, non, non, non, non, non,* NON, NON! Ziss I will not bear! Ziss I cannot endure! I get me a boy, a good boy, a painter, a real *artiste,* a genius! And what do you do? You make of him a duke! Every time it is ze same! I say, pouaaah to all dukes!"

"Oh, come now, my dear Furneaux—"

Luckily, perhaps, at this moment the royal sleigh, which had been summoned posthaste by the colonel of the

Yeomanry arrived at the riverbank with its attendant outriders. The King and his guests were all packed in, under layers of swansdown rugs. Good-bys were shouted, whips were cracked.

"I'll be back in the morning early, Dr. Furneaux!" Simon shouted. "For a long day's painting! And we'll mend the balloon."

"And collect Aunt Henrietta's tapestry!" Sophie called.

"And give a Christmas dinner to thank everybody for their help!" shouted the Duke.

Simon thought of another, sadder task, which he would hasten to perform: the small white stone on Inchmore's heathery slope with the name DIDO. And Sophie thought of the orphans at Gloober's Poor Farm to be rescued and given happy homes.

The sleigh-bells jingled, the horses began to move away in their felt slippers.

"Good night! Merry Christmas! God Save King James!"

"Merry Christmas!"

"And a Happy New Year!"

Faster and faster the procession glided off into the dark, a long trail of brilliant lights, red and gold and blue, winding along the frozen Thames to Hampton Court, until at last the glitter and the music of the bells died away, and the students went home to bed, and the mysterious peace of Christmas night descended once again upon Battersea Park.